I0618366

1. Betrayal in Cardoroth

Brand, descendant of chieftains, inched his way through the tall grass on his belly, and the peasant garb he wore became damp and filthy. He knew it would be easy to die. To live, if he could manage it, would be the hard part.

Sliding low to the muddy ground was no easy task for a big man, but regardless of the discomfort and growing risk he kept at it with all the skill and patience necessity had forced him to acquire over the last few years.

Fog, drifting from the waters of Lake Alithorin, eddied around him like ranks of slow marching phantoms. It was not daylight yet, but night was giving way to pre-dawn gray. The ghostly air dulled everything, and he used it to hide himself while he got closer to his enemies in order to hear what they said.

He was now only twenty feet away and knew that the elugs would kill him without hesitation if they saw him. Four of them squatted on the ground and whispered in guttural tones. The fifth remained apart, standing poised and alert. All wore scimitars, and Brand feared how swiftly the curved blades would flash toward his throat if he was observed.

He was as near as he could get and waited to see what would happen. These soldiers had walked away from their camp for a reason. What was it? Surely they must be meeting somebody, but who? And the camp was no mere band of raiders: it was an army. What was it doing here? Most of all, who in the northern lands of Alithoras would meet with elugs? They were everybody's enemy and servants of a great evil.

He studied them as he waited and felt a rising urge to destroy the adversaries of his people. Dawn lit the fog with the first traces of silver, and he saw droplets of water on the elugs' armor and the gray-green tinge to their dark skin. Their limbs seemed long and ungainly, but he knew they were strong and fast and had proven so during murderous raids on his homeland. He was a warrior of the Duthenor and did not back down to anything that walked on two legs. Yet it was prudent to avoid unnecessary risk, and five elugs within call of an army was sufficient reason to suppress his natural impulse.

He did not have to wait long to find out what was happening. He heard the clip-clop of a horse's hooves before the elugs did, but within moments the four squatting on the ground surged upright and spread to either side of their leader.

It was hard to tell distance in the fog, but Brand was surprised at how quickly the rider appeared. He emerged out of the shifting gray landscape on a massive black stallion, a long crimson cape trailing down his back and spilling over his mount's glossy flanks.

The rider was a man, and as he came up to the elugs he jerked viciously at the bit. The horse squealed in pain, but the cruel motion seemed more one of habit than surprise at seeing them. Nor, as Brand would have expected, did the elugs attack. They stood their ground, making no move, but tension quickened to life like flame in wind-stirred embers.

The newcomer was large and well matched to the massive proportions of his horse. When he spoke, his deep voice was muffled by the scarf warding his neck

A SPELL OF SWORDS

Robert Ryan

Copyright © 2013 Robert J. Ryan
All Rights Reserved. The right of Robert J. Ryan to be
identified as the author of this work has been asserted. All of
the characters in this book are fictitious and any resemblance
to actual persons, living or dead, is coincidental.

Cover Design by www.bookcoverartistry.com

ISBN-13 978-0-9942054-3-8
(print edition)

Trotting Fox Press

Contents

and face from the cold, but its tone of authority was apparent.

"I've come as arranged," he said without preamble, his voice coming down as though from a great height. "Now, before we go any further in this business, you will give me the gold."

The elug leader's hatred of the man was obvious. He stiffened, clearly repressing his natural instincts.

"It will be provided." As he spoke, he gestured brusquely to one of his companions who took a coarse cloth bag from beneath his tunic and shook it. By the sound, Brand guessed it contained coins, and if they were gold, it was a great deal of money.

"Is everything arranged?" asked the elug leader.

"Of course!" spat the man, seeming to take the question to mean there was some doubt about his ability. He sniffed loudly and then laughed. The authority in his voice receded and was replaced by spite. Here, thought Brand, was a man who commanded by the higher rule of another, and not by the respect of those whom he led.

"They won't know what hit them!" His eyes momentarily shone with anticipation, then grew hard and focused covetously on the bag. "Now, give me the gold."

"When will you do it?" asked the elug leader.

The newcomer dragged his gaze from the bag. "Midnight on the second night. The gate will be open, but I can only do it once."

The leader nodded to his companion, and the eyes of the elug holding the bag flared with suppressed hatred before he flung it toward the rider. Quick as a flash the man's hand swept out and caught it. Brand was astonished at his speed.

"Once is all we need," the leader said.

The rider suddenly nudged his mount forward in a menacing motion toward the elugs, and they leapt back and drew their scimitars. The massive horse then wheeled sideways and trod near to where Brand lay hidden in the grass. Just as he thought he was discovered, the rider turned back down the path he had come from. Staring back over his shoulder he sniffed loudly once more and yelled.

"Fools! All of them. But they'll soon be dead, and I have the gold I deserve. There are other cities to spend it in!" He kicked the horse into a gallop, and the massive stallion was swallowed by the fog.

Lake Alithorin

The elugs cursed viciously in their own tongue, and though Brand could not understand what they were saying, he sensed their meaning. How they wanted to kill the rider! But he served a purpose. They continued cursing as they returned to the camp, and he was soon alone. He had been witness to black treachery, and though someone trusted the rider, it showed that loyalty was only proven by actions.

His first priority must be to get away from the elug camp. Daylight was fast approaching, and he did not want to be anywhere near it when the army marched. And surely they were heading for the city of Cardoroth where he too had intended to go. The city was not only at risk from enemies without, but just as surely from foul treason within. Should he go elsewhere and avoid the danger?

His instincts always prompted his actions, and he had learned to trust them for they had saved his life many times. His decision was made even as the harsh voices of the elugs faded away. The unsuspecting people of Cardoroth were doomed unless they were warned, and he was the only one who could do so. It felt right to help them, and he sensed that his own fate was somehow linked to theirs.

He slipped along the path the rider had taken. The stallion's tracks were the deep impressions of a massive horse, shod with iron, and the shoe on the rear left leg was worn more than the others. Though no great tracker, he would know the prints if he ever saw them again.

Moving silently he set a fast pace toward Cardoroth. He was drawn into trouble he had not looked for, and it was now added to his own. Were those who had been pursuing him since he was a child nearby? Were they still hunting him down like an animal for who he was? Was it not enough that all that he loved and all that should have been his had been taken away? They wanted his life as well: but if they remained on his trail they would not find it easy to kill him. He would fight them every inch of the way.

He moved toward Cardoroth at a relentless pace. At times he jogged. At other times he walked, but always he moved forward through the long hours. It was now afternoon, and the fog was long gone.

A breeze blew from the north, and it had grown chill as the day waned. Brand looked back over his shoulder. He could not see any sign of the elugs, but he knew they were there. What he could see, and had done all day since the fog lifted, was Lake Alithorin. It shimmered like a silver basin in the wintry light. It seemed peaceful and impossibly vast. Its other side, he knew, stretched many leagues beyond his vision.

He looked ahead and studied the city of Cardoroth. For many hours it had attracted his curious glance. It was infinitely larger than any of the villages of the Duthenor. Strangely, the sun failed to light it. Its massive encircling wall, the buildings, even the cobbles of the streets were made of some dark stone that soaked up sunlight rather than reflect it. Whereas Lake Alithorin sparkled with the essence of life, Cardoroth, for all its size and the multitude of its people, looked barren.

As he neared he saw that the stone was dull red granite splashed profusely with darker flecks. The sun was lowering in the west, and the clouds were shot with a crimson glow. In the fading light the city took on the appearance of some ancient horror, a dark maw in the middle of the green fields of Alithoras, waiting to swallow a man whole. Or was he merely seeing things with the simple eyes of a villager?

Brand walked on, and in the dying light of the afternoon reached one of the gates. There were four that he knew of, one for each of the primary directions. He now faced the South Gate, open for the moment, but no doubt soon to be closed. He was about to step through when he noticed the old man.

Aranloth

The man sat in the deep shadows of the wall and leaned back against its solid bulk. An oaken staff rested idly in his weathered hands, and his flowing robes were white, as was the unruly hair on his head. His face showed wrinkles, but the skin was bright and flushed with a healthy pink. A silver diadem, almost entirely hidden by his hair, circled his brow, and it was engraved with a symbol that Brand had seen before but could not place. The old man's eyes were sea-gray, and his glance was the knowing look of a man who has seen both great joy and tragedy. They were eyes that searched the hearts of men and uncovered their secrets.

"Good afternoon, old father," Brand said politely.

8

"So it is," the stranger said. His deep voice was easy-going and smooth. "And what brings a traveler to the city of Cardoroth at this hour?"

Brand was wary. Who was this old man? Something about his voice inspired trust, but he was used to keeping his own counsel, and news of the elugs and rider must first be brought to whatever authorities he could reach.

"I'm just a wayfarer," he replied carefully, "seeking a hot meal and a warm bed for the night."

The old man smiled. "Good for you, young man. No need to tell strangers your business – even if it's important. But don't forget there are strangers who will seek to help you as well as those who will seek to hinder."

Brand shrugged his shoulders. "That's the way of the world, but I have nothing of importance to do, and no one has any reason to help or hinder me."

"Ah," the old man said, "but that's not true. You have something of great importance to do, and I intend to help."

The old man stood. He showed none of the discomfort of the elderly and straightened like a lithe warrior. When he stepped closer, Brand's hand fell to the hilt of his sword. Old the stranger may be, but power and danger were all about him like a cloak.

"It's wise to be wary, but in this case more hangs on the outcome than you guess. There's much to do and little time, so I'll tell you exactly why you've come to Cardoroth. Then I think you'll trust me, for you'll know that if I meant harm I could have already achieved it."

Brand studied the old man. He had no doubt that he could prove dangerous, but in precisely what way he was less certain. He nodded reluctantly and the stranger spoke.

"Your name is Brand, and you have fled across the great river, the Careth Nien, escaping warriors of the Duthenor who hunt you."

Brand showed no reaction. How the old man could possibly have known this he could not guess, but he was getting an inkling of an idea. Could he be a wizard, what the Duthenor called a lòhren? Was it not said that they had the sight?

"What else then, old father. Have I committed some heinous crime against my people and then fled?"

"Not unless it's a crime to be born the son of a chieftain. But your parents were murdered, and the chieftainship usurped by a rival. Those who hunt you do not serve justice but only a killer who wishes to remove a threat to his position."

Brand paled, and his blood ran like ice. He remembered as though it were only yesterday the night his parents were killed. They were kind-hearted people, deserving more from life than they got. Longing to see them once again rose within him like a wave.

The old man continued. "You're a fugitive, but your people would have you as their leader if they could. Having escaped the massacre, you were hidden by brave folk as you grew, often shifted from family to family and farm to farm because assassins searched for you ceaselessly.

You realized as you grew older that one day your luck would run out, and you would be found and killed, and those helping you murdered also. Not yet full grown but coming into manhood, you decided to leave the lands of the Duthenor to protect those who protected you. Before doing so you conceived a bold plan.

In the deep of night you stole into the hall-yard that was your home of old. Why would the guard dogs bark at someone who had played with them in better days?

You knew the ways of the old hall and picked your path among the sleeping men with slow but certain steps until you came to the usurper's chamber.

There, ever so carefully, you opened an old chest and retrieved the sword of your forefathers. With the naked blade in your hand, you were tempted to kill the usurper. Instead, you reached down and boldly slipped the ring of your father, an heirloom of chieftainship, from his finger.

He woke and gave a startled cry, but you had already fled. Men groped for their weapons all about you. 'Awake! The hall is afire!' you cried, and in the confusion slipped away.

The ruse didn't last long, and you were soon pursued. On a ridge above the village, the sickle moon riding low in the midnight sky, you gave vent to your feelings. 'I am Brand! I will return one day, and death will come with me. I am the true chieftain, and when next I see the usurper my sword will slake its thirst for justice!'

You disappeared in the wilderness, but the story of your daring grew into legend. Summer waned to autumn, and autumn turned to winter, and your enemies, ever pressing closer, forced you at last to cross the frozen river at peril of your life.

You sought to lose them by traveling the many lonely miles toward Cardoroth, of which the Duthenor have heard rumors, little guessing that you would come across an army of elugs and a treacherous meeting thereby ensnaring you in the intrigues of the city. However, involved you are, and you must decide now whether or not to accept my aid. That's how you came to Cardoroth and began talking to an old man, a lòhren entrusted with protecting a great city, who knows more than he should, but sees visions of less than he desires – including the face of the traitor."

Brand studied the old man in silence. The lòhren was impassive. It would be easier to guess what lost treasures lay hid on the deep bed of Lake Alithorin than penetrate the thoughts behind the old man's eyes. There was no way of knowing his intentions, and he was certain that to tell the wrong people his news was to court death, but his instincts prompted his actions as usual.

"As you say," he said at last, "there are those who would seek to hinder me, and I have no way of knowing if the person to whom I tell my news will be the right one, so I'll be guided by you. It's plain enough that you have some standing in the city, which I don't, so I'll see whoever in authority you think best."

The lòhren suddenly grinned. "Then we must act straightaway. I'm Aranloth, and by your trust in me you will see much in life that otherwise you would not have done."

A Wolfish Gaze

Aranloth turned briskly and walked through the gates and beneath the shadow of the great walls. Brand followed, wondering what the lòhren meant, but was soon lost in another world.

He saw green parks with statues and fountains, stone cobbled streets and many-storied buildings towering above. They made him feel as though the Duthenor were only children. What craftsmanship had his people to compare with this? Here was a civilization that was old near a thousand years before the Duthenor's wanderings brought them to the edge of the great river.

He soon tired of the spectacle though. They seemed to walk through endless streets, people milling about them, rushing like a swollen river flowing with the debris of flood.

At length the lòhren led him to an area where the gardens and buildings were even grander. There was a massive paved square, open to the sky, and the stars glittered above. Night had long since fallen on the city.

Soon they came to the palace, and though Brand had never seen one before, he recognized it for what it was. It was the tallest and most impressive building. It too was fashioned from the same red stone as the rest of the city, but it was polished and surrounded by a tall wall. They slipped through an outer gate, and the guards saluted Aranloth as he passed.

After negotiating a maze of corridors, the lòhren led him to a set of enormous doors which were carved with symbols that Brand did not recognize.

"We're here," Aranloth said. "Beyond is the one who must hear your news, the king himself, but there will be others with him. Some may be your friends, some your enemies, but watch them all closely. One of them is likely the traitor we seek."

Aranloth pushed against the doors, which swung easily at his touch, and entered the room. Brand followed. He should have guessed that the lòhren would take him to the king.

The room was large and filled with cushioned chairs and soft couches. Silk wall-hangings showed more of the strange symbols, and the floor was carpeted with animal furs. It was luxury beyond the imagination of the Duthenor, but Brand could not help wonder if living in this manner made people soft.

Out of the dozen or so men that looked toward them, one at least was not feeble. He would have been tall if he were standing but was seated at the moment on a chair facing the others. He was old; his once black hair turned silver with age, but leanness and strength were etched into his frame. He had something of the look of a wolf about him; patient, but fierce and bold when necessary.

He had to be the king, but it was one of the others who spoke first, his voice heavy with a cold.

"Welcome, Aranloth. All day we have waited for your counsel, but deprived of your presence we nevertheless managed to finalize our plans. Perhaps you had better things to do at the South Gate? Is it true that you have been sitting there since dawn? So my men there informed me, but I cursed them for fools. A lòhren, I told them, wouldn't waste his time in idleness while the city he served lay in peril."

Aranloth's expression did not change, but a cold light appeared in his eyes.

"What may be a waste to one man may yet be profitable to another, Gaspur. Had *you* gone to the gate, the day would have been wasted. I, on the other hand, have found a way to help the king in his need. It is he I serve. By his authority many are lifted up to do so; some even manage it with courtesy."

"Peace," the king said, and his voice was rich and cultured. "I don't doubt you have used your time wisely. Lòhrens, it is said, act in odd ways, but always for the good of those that they counsel. It was strange of you to remain at the gate all day while we made plans for the defense of the city. However, I should think it obvious you were waiting for someone, even if you didn't quite know when they would arrive."

At the king's words Brand felt the wolfish gaze settle on him. He stepped forward and bowed.

"Your Majesty. I'm Brand of the Duthenor. I've journeyed this winter over the frozen Careth Nien. On my way here, I espied an army of elugs, and when I left them they were camped only a day's march from the city."

14

He wanted to say more, but how was he to know whom to trust? He had thought that he might recognize the traitor by his size and dress, but at least half the men in the room were large, and save for the king, all wore crimson capes. It must be part of the uniform of the captains of the army.

Gaspur laughed. It was not the reaction Brand expected.

"It seems that Aranloth's wait was wasted after all. Is this outlander a simpleton? Does he think we're unaware that an elug army approaches?"

Brand went red. He came here to help, and to be called a simpleton for his pains was insulting. What was going on? What was the background between Aranloth and Gaspur that ignited such enmity against a stranger?

"The deed was well done, Gaspur," the king said in his rich voice, "even if we already knew of the army coming down from the northern mountains. A good deed should not be rebuked, and I offer my thanks."

Brand composed himself. The king, if no one else, was courteous. He smiled though as he heard the words about the elugs coming from the north: his news was not stale after all.

"A simpleton you call me," he said to Gaspur, "but at least I know north from south. You know of an army coming from the northern mountains, but the army I saw was coming from the *south*."

The room broke into uproar. This was indeed news, and not good news either. He was questioned much thereafter by the king, whose wolfish stare bored into him, gleaning details of numbers, emblems and shield shapes and drawing deductions from them with quick intelligence.

Brand kept his words to a minimum and said nothing of his own background and found no opportunity to warn the king of the traitor in front of the captains.

At length, the king finished. "Well, you've brought us valuable information, and I'd like to repay you for your service."

Aranloth spoke before Brand had a chance to say anything.

"Brand is seeking to stay in Cardoroth," he said. "It may be well to allow him to continue to serve. Perhaps, given the perils we face, it would be wise to employ him as a soldier."

The king's eyes narrowed. Not in suspicion, thought Brand, but in recognition that the lòhren rarely spoke to no purpose.

"What!" roared Gaspur. "How can a Duthenor join the finest soldiers in Alithoras? What skills will an outlander have? Hiring a shepherd won't help us fight elugs!"

Brand felt an urge to show Gaspur exactly what fighting skills the Duthenor had, but he restrained himself and spoke only to the king. He had a sudden idea.

"My Lord, it's true that I come to the city an untested man, and though I may be an outlander, it's not clear to me that living in stone halls with soft chairs and silk covered beds is better training for a warrior than living in the open fields and secret woods of Alithoras. But I've done more than tend sheep in my time. I can fight as well as any among the Duthenor, and they are a strong people. I'm also very good with horses, and if it pleases you, I should like to become a soldier of Cardoroth."

The king looked long at Aranloth, who stood quietly leaning against his oaken staff.

"Very well then," he said. "A soldier you'll become, and we'll find a place for you among those who care for the cavalry. Captain Caldor will take you to his barracks shortly and give you instructions."

Brand bowed. "Thank you, my Lord."

He was pleased with himself at how things had turned out. He was now a soldier of Cardoroth, and what's more, he'd created a chance to find the black stallion. If he couldn't trace the traitor by his clothes then the horse would do just as well. Then he would find a better opportunity to tell the king the rest of his story. It had only been a brief meeting, but Brand was impressed. The king was a leader that a man could follow, and already he sensed loyalty sparking to life.

The Hunt

Caldor took him to the barracks adjacent to the Northern Gate. These were a series of connected stone buildings forming a square around an inner courtyard. The style was less grand than many other buildings in the city but not unattractive, and to Brand the stables, eating hall and courtyard used for training were far better than anything among the Duthenor.

Caldor spoke little and left him in a room he was to share with eleven other men. These were veteran soldiers, and they looked at him disdainfully. That he was an outlander was obvious, but it was just as apparent that he was very poor. Even rough soldiers from Cardoroth dressed in finer clothes, and he felt their stares.

Brand waited. He knew the time old testing of the new recruit was about to begin. These were hard men in difficult times: never mind the army; they would establish for themselves where he fitted into their ranking system.

A raw boned lump of a man walked over. He had a red beard and a pallid scar above his left eye. He looked at Brand in disgust, but his words were addressed to his companions.

"The captain's not real bright, lads. Last time he gave us a boy who kept pricking himself with his own sword; couldn't manage to get it up in front of his body when the elugs ambushed our patrol though. This time he's really gone too far – he's given us a girl!"

The soldiers roared with laughter. When the noise subsided Brand spoke steadily.

"If I were a girl, I'd stay clear of you. Your face looks like the wrong end of a donkey with the runs."

The man turned crimson and stepped forward with clenched fists. Brand swung a punch from the hip. It was fast and took his opponent by surprise. One moment the soldier was standing, and the next there was a mighty crack, and he fell to the floor like a dropped sack of grain. He lay unmoving while a bright stream of blood flowed from his nose.

Brand looked around him. Would the others now turn on him? He watched while somebody fetched a towel and helped the bearded man up. It was one of the other men who broke the silence. "Well, I reckon you don't punch like no girl."

That was all that was said. These were tough men, but they were fair.

Brand lay down in a bunk, pulled the blankets around him, and promptly went to sleep. As he drifted off, he wondered what the morning would bring. Could he track down the stallion and its treacherous rider? Could he discover which gate would be opened to the elugs?

Dawn came, but Brand had been up an hour before it arrived. He had been given a burnished helm, hard-soled leather boots, gray trousers and tunic. Captain Caldor, his recently appointed leader, wanted to give him a new sword as well; the shorter and thicker type favored in Cardoroth, but Brand refused. The blade of his forefathers was all he wished for. That, and to identify the man who intended to betray the inhabitants of an entire city.

Now in his new clothes he was walking through the stables and checking on the horses, mucking out stalls and helping with the feeding. His companion, showing him what was to be done, was the raw boned man that he had knocked down last night. His nose was swollen, and one of his eyes was a black pool.

Ruthlaan, for so he introduced himself, said little. When he spoke it was as though the events of last night had not occurred, and Brand left it at that also.

During the course of their work he spotted the massive black stallion. There could only be one horse like that in Cardoroth, and checking its tracks in the sand-lined stall, he saw as he expected that the shoe on the rear left leg was worn down more than the others.

"This one's a beauty," he said to Ruthlaan, stroking its long neck.

His companion grunted. "That's the captain's very own horse, that is. It's fast as the wind but a mean and nasty piece of work. Kick your head off if you're not careful."

Brand did not answer. He could now put a name to the traitor, though he liked Captain Caldor and it was hard to picture him consorting with elugs, but the evidence was there. Now, he must work out what to do about it. His thoughts were interrupted by distant yelling.

Ruthlaan went out to see what was happening and came back a few moments later.

"We better finish up. We'll be wanted on the walls soon. The elugs are in view, and there'll be fighting before the morning is finished."

The Storm Breaks

They heard as they worked the commotion going on all about them. Women were hurrying along the streets, soldiers were racing to and fro, and there was a sense of urgency. Brand did not detect signs of panic though. These people had been through sieges before.

Their chores passed swiftly, and when finished, Brand and Ruthlaan joined the rest of their troop on the walls. The men had not seen any action yet as they were being held as reserves. The fighting had started though and wave after wave of elugs had rushed toward the defenses. Most charges had been broken by an unremitting hail of arrows. A few had reached the next stage where the elugs were able to throw scaling ladders and grappling hooks against the wall and climb the ramparts. These were soon slashed down by the sharp blades of the soldiers.

One group, particularly fierce, was now coming up the ladders like swarming spiders. They burst through the defenders and cut and thrust with wickedly curved swords while men fell about them.

Suddenly the tall figure of Captain Gaspur was among them. His sword flickered delicate death at one moment, and the next swept in mighty arcs hewing off heads and limbs. One elug, clambering over the wall, threw a spear at him. The long length of wood shivered through the air with the force of the throw. Gaspur turned, saw the elug, but had no time for evasive action. Instead, his free hand flickered out and swatted the spear away so that it clattered harmlessly onto the stone. Then in moments the soldiers rallied, and the elugs were killed.

At dusk the last wave of attackers had been rebuffed. Brand followed his troop toward the barracks and paused when he saw Aranloth stride toward him.

The lòhren came to a halt and leaned on his oaken staff, appraising him with those sea-gray eyes.

"Well, you now look almost like you were born in Cardoroth. Have you discovered anything of note?"

"Only this," answered Brand. "Watching battles is much less interesting than drawing steel and matching your skill against enemies."

"That may be so," the lòhren said, "but all the swordsmanship in the world will not save us from treason."

"Very well then," Brand said reluctantly. "I've discovered this. The owner of the black stallion is Captain Caldor."

Aranloth frowned. "Are you sure?"

Brand looked at him. He did not wish to be sure, but he was.

"I may not be a lòhren, but I know horses. It was one and the same. And the captain owns him and fits the looks of the rider that I saw. He's a big man and wears a long crimson cape. What's more, he's Captain of the North Gate."

"I don't like it," Aranloth said, "but evidence is evidence."

He leaned on his staff and thought for a few moments.

"At the moment you're the only witness against him. As a stranger, he'll cast suspicion on your word, and others will come to his defense. If we're to prove his guilt beyond doubt we must catch him in the act. If I don't misjudge the king, that's the only evidence he'll accept against one of his most trusted."

Brand frowned. "It's a pity that not all men show the same loyalty as the king does."

"That may be," Aranloth said, "but the king has a greater heart than most. Anyway, midnight of the second night is the hour of testing, and I'll tell him what you held back. He'll no doubt want to see things with his own eyes and will come with his personal guard. We'll go to your barracks and keep watch. Then we shall see what we shall see."

The Curse of Cardoroth

The lòhren left him, and Brand went back to the barracks and slept deeply. The next morning was dim and eerie. Fog, almost thick enough to cup in the hands, had swept out from Lake Alithorin during the night, and men could see no more than a dozen paces ahead. It felt like the clammy hands of a host of dead men reaching toward life, and everywhere the red stone of the city seemed to glisten with drops of blood.

Brand stood atop the battlements and listened to the talk of the soldiers. Some spoke of signs and portents, and how blood would be spilled during the day. Others whispered of the ancient curse of Cardoroth; of how the king was doomed to be assassinated and the city destined to fall in blood and ash. Brand did not know anything about the prophecy, but he knew this: he and many others were armed, and if the city were to be saved it would be by men who fought for their home; who struggled with all their mortal strength and with their wits as well.

His regiment was allocated to defend another part of the wall this morning, but there was no fighting. While the fog was thick there was little chance of any attack from the elugs. It would be madness to attempt scaling the walls. Everything was wet and slippery, and the lack of visibility would hinder attackers as much as defenders.

At noon, he and his men were ordered off the walls. The fog was thinning to wisps and blowing away on a cold breeze driving from the north.

Brand was disappointed. He had not yet been involved in even the smallest skirmish or had a chance to show these city folk how the Duthenor fought. He was in the barracks when battle broke out once again and cursed his luck. Throughout the long afternoon all he could hear were the sounds of fighting; the screams of the dying, the curses and swearing of hard-pressed men and the bloodcurdling yells of elugs.

At dusk, the last attack was rebuffed, and many men started to come back to the barracks. Only a reserve was left on the walls, sufficient to sound the alarm and hold off any surprise night attack until reinforcements came. Brand decided it was time to get some sleep. While men caroused in the barracks, celebrating that they were still alive, he lay his head on the cloak that he used as a pillow and slept. When he awoke, an hour or so before midnight, all was silent and still. The lights were out, and the men turned into their beds.

Fire and Blood!

He dressed swiftly and went to the now empty eating hall. Pulling up a chair near the door he also had a good view of the gate out of the window.

He did not have long to wait. One by one, so as to avoid any chance of suspicion, soldiers of the king's guard came to the door. Brand silently let them in. Soon twenty-five men stood about him, and last to enter were the lòhren and the king.

The king was dressed as a common soldier, and Brand could see by the look in his eye that he felt both anxiety and excitement.

Aranloth pulled up a chair and joined him by the window. "I saw Ruthlaan sporting a black eye today."

Brand smiled. "I noticed that too. Someone must have hit him mighty hard!"

Aranloth nodded. "He gets a bit big for his boots sometimes, that one. He's a good fighter though."

Brand would have said more, but at that moment Captain Caldor came into view. He was walking down the street, and they would not have known him except for the dull light coming from a brazier used by the six gate guards for warmth. Two of them stood to attention near the gate while the remaining four sat on chairs a little way behind them.

The king's guard grew silent, and Brand sensed the keen attention of the city's leader and glanced up. There was a new glint in the king's eyes. They held an even harder edge than normal, and Brand instinctively knew this man lived for one thing only; to see the city well protected and prosperous. He did not take kindly to those who dealt with the people's enemies for their own reward.

Captain Caldor and the seated soldiers exchanged some joke. Brand could not hear what it was, but then one of the men got up and offered his chair. The soldiers were gambling to while away the hours, and one of the men threw dice, one at a time, to the captain. Caldor made a clumsy attempt to catch them, and they spilled from his hands to the red cobbles. He laughed as he reached down to pick them up.

Brand watched, and a sense of unease swept over him. What was wrong? He cast his mind back over what had led to this point. There was no doubting the horse. He knew it by its looks and also by its tracks. Likewise, there was no doubt that Captain Caldor was its owner. So he must be the traitor. *But what if he weren't?* What if somebody else had ridden the horse that night?

Suddenly, he knew what was disturbing him. The traitor had spoken to the elugs and then, when the bag of gold was thrown to him he caught it with speed and dexterity. Caldor had never moved like that in his life! Who then was the traitor? It had to be one of the captains, for only they wore the crimson cloak. But which one?

Brand remembered what had happened on the battlements yesterday. He closed his eyes and pictured the long spear snaking through the air and the speed and skill of Gaspur as his hand flicked out and swatted it aside. Then he remembered the loud sniff of the traitor and the scene in the room with the king and his councilors came back to him. Gaspur had been suffering from a cold!

Brand suddenly stood, and his chair fell back behind him. He turned to the king. "My Lord, forgive me! I've been a fool. My instincts told me the traitor wasn't Caldor, and I should've listened. There's no time to tell you how I made the mistake, but Caldor's innocent. The traitor is Gaspur! We shouldn't be here but at the South Gate. Fire and blood! I hope it's not too late!"

Thunder in the Streets

Brand rushed to the stables. He realized he left turmoil in his wake, but now he knew where he had to go. The others would follow as they could. First, he must

25

find a horse. The fastest he knew was Caldor's black stallion: the same one Gaspur must have ridden so as not to be recognized on his treacherous errand.

Brand went to his stall but did not waste time saddling him. He whispered in his ear, stroked his long sleek neck and was flashing out the door just as the others came into the stables. He left them behind: lòhren, king and soldiers all.

"To the South Gate or the city is lost!" he yelled.

He flew through the city as though the horse was winged. The clatter of hooves on cobbles thundered up the long streets between tall buildings, and sparks flew from the iron-shod hooves. People were woken from their sleep, but by the time their senses cleared the horse had passed, and all that was left was a distant rattle like the remnants of a storm in the far hills.

Brand raced on and fear rode with him. Was he too late? Would he reach the gate only to see that the elugs had already taken it? If so, he would sell his life dearly somewhere on the red streets of the city.

The black stallion galloped like the wind, and Brand knew he had made the right choice. The horse had heart! His sides were flecked with foam, and his mouth was wide open, his great lungs straining for air. Up hills, down hills, turning through twisted streets he sped through the sleeping city and then finally came to the gate.

What he saw as he swung down and drew his sword was something to bring dread to all who lived in the city. Six watchmen lay slumped on the ground, drugged or poisoned. Gaspur was putting his shoulder to the right half of the gate and that side was swinging open. The left remained locked and bolted into the ground by a black iron rod as thick as a man's leg. Teeming behind were scores of elugs.

As Brand came up Gaspur turned around, but not soon enough. Brand felled him with a blow to the side of his helmet with the hilt of his sword, and he fell to the ground with a heavy thump. But it was too late. Some of the elugs were now pulling the gate open while others poured through.

Brand braced his legs and swung. His sword cut the air like the claws of a wild beast brought to bay, delivering death with each strike. Elugs died as they stood, unable to spread out because of the warrior blocking their way. He fought them two to one, but as he slew them another would madly leap into place. He was cut on the arms and legs, and blood streamed down his limbs. His helm was knocked off by a mighty blow that sent him crashing to his knees, but he stood again without a backward step and dealt death once more.

The elugs pressed harder. They seemed numberless and were filled with the glee of bloodlust and fired by the knowledge the city they hated was within their grasp.

One man could not stop them. Not for long, but each second that Brand held them up was a chance for help to arrive. His sight was narrowed by the vicious blow that dislodged his helm. His arms were growing heavy as lead, and he was dizzy and barely able to see the elugs coming against him.

The end was near when the elugs made way for one of their champions. He was taller and bigger than the others, holding a great black mace in one hand and a short dagger in the other. His muscles shifted beneath his tunic like ocean waves rolling to the shore. The huge mace was lifted and came swinging down at Brand's head with enough force to flatten a mountain.

Brand did not try to block the blow. The mace was too heavy, and the strength of the elug too much. Nor could he move back to avoid the stroke for to do so would open a gap through which his opponents would stream. He did the only thing he could. Stepping forward he shouldered his attacker. He took a blow to his head but knew it was the handle of the mace rather than the deadly end. He felt his own impact against the elug, and then they clinched each other in a mighty struggle. He felt the dagger stab against his side, but his chain mail protected him.

The elug's arm reached lower, the dagger seeking a spot near his thigh to drain the blood from one of the main arteries. Brand dropped his sword, which was useless at such close quarters. With both hands he gripped the elug, and then his opponent took a step backwards and lost balance. Brand took his chance and strained every muscle. He picked the elug up, his enemy still seeking to stab him, but before he found a vulnerable spot Brand heaved and used the last of his strength to throw his opponent. The elug measured his length through the air and crashed into his companions. They went down but came up howling for blood.

Even as they recovered Brand bent down and snatched up his sword once more. He braced his legs for the final charge, but it never came. All about him were the shouts of men and the rattle of hooves. The elugs scattered as archers began to shower them with arrows, and the gate was closed.

Brand of the Duthenor

Brand turned and leaned on his sword. With dim vision he saw Aranloth and the king getting down from their horses. Gaspur had been dragged to the side of the gate and was now conscious again. Two soldiers pinned his arms behind his back.

Brand bowed on wobbly legs to the king. "My Lord: that was how the Duthenor fight!"

The wolfish eyes of the king studied the piled bodies of elugs about the gate, and his expression held a hint of awe.

"Indeed," he said slowly, "if we had more Duthenor like you we could purge the northern mountains of elugs. But you have rid us of enough foes for one day. You have saved the kingdom by your own hand. Speak, and I will give you any gift in my power."

Brand laughed. "That's easy, my Lord. One day I hope to go home and right the wrongs inflicted on my people. Until that time I ask only for this – the black stallion but for whose great heart the city would have been destroyed and a place among your soldiers until I return to the Duthenor. And," he continued after a sideways glance at Gaspur, "as you now need a new captain, I offer my services."

The king laughed. "Many would have asked for more, but you ask enough! I'm sure I can offer Caldor sufficient money to give you the horse, and you have a place among the soldiers as long as you wish. As for the captaincy, I would like to do so, but there are many men who have served me for years and sworn their loyalty to me before you were born. I cannot lightly set that aside and promote you above them."

The king glanced at the lòhren. "What is your counsel on this, Aranloth? It seems, as ever, that your wisdom runs deep. It was through you that Brand was allowed to serve, and that has turned out for the best."

Aranloth considered before answering. "My Lord, there is much in the future that is hidden to me, but I see this. Cardoroth is in great peril. This has not been the first attempt on the city, nor will it be the last. Danger and treachery are afoot. Men have sworn loyalty to you;

29

men such as Gaspur. But Brand has proven it with his actions. Nay, he has proven it with the very lifeblood flowing from his veins! He will be of great service to you, and the men will follow him. He has luck, and he will have their respect after tonight. Who else but one of the wild Duthenor could have held off so many elugs?"

"So be it then," the king said solemnly. "Brand of the Duthenor, I name you a captain in Cardoroth's army."

Then heedless of the blood splattered over Brand, he embraced him. The soldiers cheered, and through the dizzy mist sweeping over him, Brand felt a wave of euphoria.

2. King's Reward

Brand took a deep breath and entered the room.

It was dim in the king's chamber. Heavy drapes hung over the windows. They blotted out the world and expunged its light. Beyond the embroidered hangings and densely plastered walls, people laughed, danced, ran, shouted and bustled through their everyday lives. Inside, grief held sway: heads sagged, speech was hushed, and eyes gazed blankly. Even the white-smocked healers, bearded old men attended by young assistants, remained quiet and respectful – or sullen in defeat.

Aranloth sat on a cushioned chair beside the king's bed. His eyes were half-closed and his shoulders slumped. The pale oaken staff that signaled his profession leaned through the crook of an arm. He muttered elusive words in a foreign tongue. Words of magic.

Brand frowned. Something was amiss. No spell could recall the king's spirit. Why did the lòhren expend his power?

The sharp scent of healing concoctions crowded the air: frankincense, wild-harvested honey, myrrh and cedar wood. Brand recognized them and many others, but it was the clean fragrance of the cedar that quickened memory to life. His mind flew back to childhood, to the high limestone hills of his homeland during crisp autumn days. It woke yearnings in him: for his own people, for his old life that was lost, for a simpler way of living that did not involve his sword.

His blade was at the king's service though. Gilhain had won his loyalty by trusting him, a stranger to the city of Cardoroth, when the less charitable offered nothing but disdain. The king had given him a chance as a soldier and later promoted him to captain. The years might grow old, but Brand would never forget. He looked at him now, shrouded by opulent bedclothes, his eyes closed, his skin gray, and felt helpless. Bravery and skill at arms were useless. For the first time he wished to be more than a warrior.

The queen left the side of her dark-haired granddaughter, who wept quietly, and approached him. Though grief marked her face, she was composed and veiled her gaze. Yet he glimpsed a flicker of rage.

He had heard not an hour since of King Gilhain's passing. Rumor hurried through the city: the queen had sworn to identify and execute the assassin who had poisoned him. Nothing would stop her.

Brand bowed. When he lifted his head, she bent her gaze upon him, and he felt the force of her iron-like will.

"You have heard of the king's death?"

"Yes," he said. She had summoned him to this room. Unexpectedly. The less he spoke, the sooner she would reveal why.

Her scrutiny of him did not waver. "It is not true."

He glanced at Gilhain. The king was still. Nor was there any sign of breathing. His skin was gray, his lips blue. Brand had seen slain men, more often than he wished to remember, and knew the king was dead. And yet ... and yet what did he know of poisons? Certainly, Aranloth worked to a purpose.

Hope kindled in his eyes, and there was a catch in his voice.

"The lòhren keeps him alive?"

She gave a slight nod. "Yes. But only just. The healers have failed – they have no cure for the poison that ravages his body."

Even as she spoke Brand saw the king spasm.

"How long can Aranloth do this?"

The queen turned her gaze toward the lòhren. There was something in her expression that Brand could not read. Gratitude? Respect? Awe?

She looked back. "You can see how greatly it taxes him. The king yet lives, but will pass before midnight."

Her eyes hardened with determination, and Brand knew she would now reveal the reason for his summons.

"I misspoke, before," she said. "The healers have no remedy. Except Barathar."

She beckoned over a bearded old man. He in turn made a curt gesture to a young woman. Brand sensed the healer's heavy-lidded gaze dismiss him as of little consequence. The woman stood a pace behind her master, eyes downcast.

"Barathar and Arell have encountered this poison before. He understands its nature … and knows its remedy. There is a plant that grows near Lake Alithorin. It favors cliff sides." The queen's voice wavered. "It alone can save the king."

The healer brushed pale fingers, each glinting with gold rings, down his smock. He looked at all of them in turn with dark eyes.

"It's known to the wise as *karanthrot*."

Brand did not like him. In his experience, those who were keen to impress others with their knowledge knew the least. He ignored his dislike and thought quickly. Lake Alithorin was not far away, and there remained a chance to save Gilhain. Nothing accounted for his unexpected summoning though. He waited.

The queen continued. "I trust you, Brand. You've proven your loyalty. I want you to go with Arell and fetch the plant."

Brand considered the situation. He understood why Arell must go; someone had to identify the karanthrot, and the old man was too frail for a rigorous journey. There was more, though.

"Why not send a troop? If something went wrong ... there would be others to finish the mission."

The queen nodded. "Yes. That was my initial thought, too. But in this case, secrecy is better."

She pursed her lips and considered her next words carefully. "Cardoroth, and the king, have many enemies. But only a member of our household could have poisoned him."

That was likely enough. Brand knew something of assassins.

The queen paused and clasped her hands together.

"That's why I started the rumor of the king's death. Let them think they succeeded! It will give you a better chance. If I sent a troop, word would spread rapidly, and they might contrive another attempt on his life. More likely, they would try to kill Arell. Even a company of soldiers couldn't protect her from a far off archer or a knife hurled from the crowd."

Brand understood. The king's life depended on Arell ... and her safety on him. The queen's strategy was sound, yet they all knew that his summoning might have been marked. The girl, dressed in well-worn shoes and a plain linen dress, stood in the shadow of her master. She was quiet and meek as the people of Cardoroth expected of a girl, but he liked that she showed no fear.

He glanced one last time at Gilhain, and then bowed.

"I'll return with karanthrot – or die trying."

He strode from the chamber and Arell followed. Speed was essential. Not only for the king, but to preempt any attempt to waylay them. The assassin need not know the exact purpose of Brand's summons; his swift departure with a healer's assistant was enough to draw suspicion.

Lake Alithorin

Within the hour they passed through the city gate. He rode his favorite black stallion, and Arell was mounted on a sorrel mare. She struck purposefully for the location where she expected to find the karanthrot.

They soon saw the lake. It glittered in the light of late morning, though fog gathered along its shores and reached long arms into the surrounding pine forests. Its other side lay many leagues beyond his vision.

He looked back and studied Cardoroth. It was far larger than the villages of his homeland. Its encircling wall, buildings, and even the cobbles of its streets were of a dark stone. He was more used to thatched huts, but the land of his youth was sweet, and his heart suddenly ached for it.

He thought about his companion as they approached the lake. Arell spoke seldom but seemed calm and assured. She could not be more different from her master, a pompous man who appeared the type to cover ignorance with unnecessary displays of knowledge.

In the villages of his homeland girls learned to fight, plough fields, hunt, heal or do whatever necessity demanded. In Cardoroth, the people shunned female healers as witches and generally expected little of their women except those of noble birth, such as the queen. Arell probably had to endure Barathar to eke out a living, at least in her chosen profession. Judging by her threadbare clothes, he paid her little. It went against Brand's grain, but he was in no position to change it. Trying would only reinforce that he was a foreigner and get him into trouble. It might even ensure he never received a promotion.

The road dwindled to a sandy trail that snaked beneath tall pines. It grew dark. The air, humid and still, stank of rot. Orange fungus flowered in lush growths on fallen timber, and long fingers of gray-green moss trailed from overhead branches. They slowed. In the murk of the pinewood it felt like hostile eyes watched their every move.

Tendrils of mist reached phantom-like through the trees. The lake was close, and Arell found a steep path down a rock-strewn bank. At its bottom the trees gave way to a narrow track.

They rode northward, the sandy lakeshore on their left, and the steepening bank on their right. It soon became a cliff. The rock-face beetled above: craggy, slick with moisture, and its high top hidden by mist.

Arell ran her sharp gaze over it. "Look for something red."

Brand smiled to himself. He liked her no-nonsense attitude and that she knew exactly what she was doing.

He searched hard and long, but she spotted the karanthrot first. Her long arm shot out and pointed.

"There!"

Brand saw it, a little clump of green and red nestled within a crack in the rocks. It was only thirty feet above them, but a difficult climb. He dismounted, handed the reins to Arell, and studied the cliff.

"Broken bones are easy to set," she said. "But be careful anyway."

He admired her confidence. Yet she also seemed worried for his safety. The soldiers he knew would only have joked, and her concern touched a chord in him.

He commenced to climb. It was slow going, yet he resisted the urge to hasten. There would be no second chance if he fell.

There were handholds in rough crevices, and his boots gained purchase on outthrusts of hard stone. He ascended, oblivious to the loud hum of insects in the distance, the sweat that beaded on his forehead or the trickles of blood on his hands from sharp-edged rocks.

It was his protected foot that slipped, though. The leather sole of a shoe, that had seemed secure against a rock, gave way and he dangled from two arms, little more than his fingers keeping him in place. He groaned with strain and heard a gasp from below.

Agony shot through his hands, and fear crashed against his mind. He ignored everything and concentrated only on finding a little ledge or hollow where he could secure the toe of a boot and help support his weight. His seeking feet found nothing.

He could not carry his weight by his arms forever. Better to take a risk now, while there was still strength in them, than later. He swung his body carefully from side to side and then reached out with a hand for a large crevice where he could improve his grip.

Rocks and dirt showered down the cliff face, and his chest and legs scraped over the ragged surface, but his new grip held and he found a foothold as well. He stayed still, the only movement the heaving of his chest and stomach, which pressed into the stone as he breathed. He stayed that way for some time, and then he began to climb again.

He came within reach of the karanthrot. It was a small plant, broad of leaf and with succulent, crimson stalks. There were several flowers too, the petals cream with a pink center. He was not sure which part contained the antidote: stalk, leaf or flower, so he pulled the whole plant. There were barely any roots, and it came away easily. He stuffed it into a pocket of his tunic.

He climbed down slowly and let out a long sigh when he reached the bottom. Arell flashed him a brilliant smile, though there was concern in her eyes, and then threw him his reins and sprang upon her horse.

Race to the King

They raced along the narrow track between bank and lake.

Mist swirled ahead of them. Brand, in the lead, unexpectedly saw a tall man on the path. He was dressed in black, hooded, and with a long sword sheathed at his side. In his hands was a bow, strung and fitted with a steel-headed arrow.

The archer stood poised and alert, a tethered horse some way behind him. Was he a hunter? No. The assassin had learned of their mission or followed on mere suspicion.

Brand could not turn on the narrow trail. Nor could he ride up the steep bank or into the water. The archer knew it. He raised his weapon, and Brand did the only thing left to him. He urged his horse onward and tried to run the figure down. It was a desperate ploy. The assassin could not miss, but maybe Arell would get a chance to break through and escape.

The great stallion responded. Loose sand and rock churned beneath its iron-shod hooves. The archer fired. Brand, leaning low in the saddle, glimpsed the long arrow streak toward him and flinched. He felt a hammer-like blow in the bunched muscles between his shoulder and neck that nearly knocked him to the ground. Searing pain shot through him as the horse surged forward.

The assassin, suddenly aware of his danger, tried to leap off the path into the water, but the black stallion crashed into him.

Brand groaned in pain as he pulled up his horse. The arrow was stuck in his flesh, but he twisted and looked over his shoulder. The bowman staggered to his feet while the girl, quick as dancing flame, rode close and struck at his neck with a flashing hand.

Only after Brand saw the spurt of blood did he notice the slender blade in her grip. She had precisely targeted an artery, and the man reeled back, fell and swiftly died while his hands tried futilely to stem the flow.

The assassin's hood had fallen back, but Brand did not recognize him. The queen would have to have his body retrieved for identification.

Brand watched Arell through the haze of his agony. She came to him swiftly, helped him dismount and laid him gently on his side. She studied his wound professionally, working with speed and efficiency, and then prepared strips of cloth.

She looked him in the eyes. "It could be worse," she said.

Brand spoke through gritted teeth. "It hurts ... like the blazes!"

"But you're alive to feel it."

He waited as she ordered her thoughts.

"The arrow-head has nearly pierced right though you," she said. "I can feel it bulging out the skin on the other side of the wound."

He had seen arrow wounds treated before and prepared himself.

"If I pull the arrow, you might bleed profusely."

He nodded.

"If I don't pull it, you won't be able to ride. It'll be a long wait for help to arrive."

"Do it," he said. "The sooner the wound bleeds the less chance of festering."

Arell appraised him, assessing his ability to endure pain.

"Hold still," she said. For a moment her eyes showed sympathy, but there was no lessening of her confidence. She steadied the shaft and with deft movements of her knife shaved away the fletching.

When she was done, she looked at him once more in warning. Brand clenched his jaw, and she pushed the arrow through smoothly. He groaned and fainted. When he woke a few moments later, pain roared through him, but the arrow was gone and cloth staunched his bleeding.

His mind cleared. "Take the karanthrot and go," he said. "I'll be alright now. The king needs you more."

She shook her head. "I'm not leaving you here. The wound needs cleaning, proper dressings and an unguent to stop it from turning bad. The quicker all that's done the better."

She helped him up. Once mounted, he felt as though he might just manage to stay on. The pain was lessening, and his sight had cleared. He saw the concern on her face and attempted a smile to ease her worry.

"Let's go!" he said. "But if I fall, take the antidote and save the king. You can come back for me."

She did not answer. Nor did he fall on the journey back. As evening shot red shafts of light against Cardoroth's buildings they thundered through the city gate. By the time long shadows glided down the streets they raced over cobbles, driving sparks against the blackness. It was night when they rushed through the palace and came breathless to the king's chamber.

40

Gilhain yet lived. The lòhren still muttered words of power but was slumped across the chair like a felled tree. All eyes looked their way as Barathar and the queen hastened toward them. She noted Brand's bloodied tunic, but he spoke first.

"We have it!"

He pulled the karanthrot from his pocket, which he had broken down to its components of stem, leaf and flower. He looked hard at Barathar. Were his guesses about the healer near the mark? He decided to find out, whatever the consequences, and held forth his cupped hands.

"Which part contains the antidote?"

Barathar glanced at Arell. "My assistant knows – she'll dispense it."

"You're the healer," Brand said. "Come! Heal the king."

He pushed his hands forward. "Choose!"

Barathar reached out a tentative hand. It trembled, and he snatched it back. His mouth opened, but he found no words to speak.

Brand turned to Arell. "Will you tend the king, healer?"

She looked at him with wide eyes. He saw her hesitation as she realized that he would make enemies by this action. He pushed his hands forward, and she took the opportunity he offered. She plucked only the thick stem and moved purposefully to the bed.

The queen's sharp eyes bored into Barathar. "Why did you refuse to heal your king?"

The healer stepped back.

"He can't," Brand said. "Arell obviously knows more. She's the true healer, and though I'd trust my life to her

41

skill, the people in this city look only to bearded old men to tend them."

Barathar spoke at last. "You might trust her, but few would pay a hedgerow witch to heal them. I took her in my service, shared some profits with her. And this is my reward?" He shot a venomous glance at Arell's back. "Where's her loyalty?"

Brand grunted and watched as she squeezed juice from the karanthrot stem into the king's mouth.

"Loyalty is earned," he said, "not traded like a trinket in the market."

The king coughed. His labored breathing eased, and it seemed that he drifted into sleep rather than the shadow-dreams of fever.

The lòhren's muttering gradually softened and then stopped. He straightened in his chair; the oaken staff dropped from his hands and clattered on the floor.

"The king will live," he rasped. Then he buried his head in his hands.

Light shone in the queen's eyes. She turned them on Barathar, and they narrowed to dark slits.

"Brand has ensured the girl will not want for patients now. She healed the king and word will spread. You, and many others, will lose clients to her. Starting with my family."

The white-smocked men in the room shuffled uncomfortably. They cast brooding glances at Brand, but he did not give a damn what they thought. He looked at Arell and she flashed him a smile. His decision might cost him, but he would live with it.

3. The Helm of the Duthenor

Brand looked across the table and studied the man who sat opposite. He knew only three things about him. His name was Felargin. For joining a risky venture he offered as reward something Brand wanted. And the man intended to kill him before he could claim it.

The usual tavern noises were about them; sudden laughter in response to jests, loud speech and the clatter of empty mugs collected by nimble-fingered maids. Brand allowed none of them to distract him.

The first two things he was supposed to know, but not the third. He might have come from the wild lands of the Duthenor to the city of Cardoroth, but that did not mean he was stupid. Felargin had agreed too readily to give the Helm of the Duthenor as payment from the treasure; an artifact that would outweigh Brand's share of the enterprise. Also, there was something in the man's eyes that did not spark to life regardless of his easy smile.

Felargin leaned over the table, his knobby arms devoid of muscle. "Are we agreed, then?"

Brand sipped his ale. "Very well, I'll meet you and the others at the South Gate in three days."

Felargin leaned back. "Make it at dawn," he said. "We'll be waiting for you." He rose and walked out to the street on legs like sticks.

Brand sat alone in deep thought. Had he just agreed to a venture that would cost him his life? Perhaps, yet the risk was worth it. What warrior among his people would pass up the chance to obtain a legendary heirloom of the Duthenor? And though he did not trust Felargin, it was hard to imagine what threat the weakling could pose. It would be prudent to consult Aranloth though. The lòhren was a friend, wise in the ways of the world and adept at magic, and that was something to take advantage of.

He was going to spend the next few hours in quiet contemplation of the task ahead. At least, that was his intention. It was clear from the expression on the face of the man who now approached that he would not be left alone to do so.

The man sauntered over and sat down uninvited in Felargin's chair. He was tall, with multiple scars running along his arms and a single white line across his neck. He did not carry a sword and Brand took him for a knife fighter. It was something to keep in mind.

"You and that skinny feller seem to have had a nice chat."

Brand frowned. "Hardly cause for comment at an inn."

"I don't much like your tone," answered the newcomer.

"If you don't like it, there are plenty of other tables to sit at," Brand said pointedly.

The man laughed. "You'd like that," he said. He tapped a finger against his nose. "I have a feel for things from time to time. I know when things are happening. That Felargin has been hanging around here a lot. Won't tell nobody what he's about though. But I got an idea it's something big. I've heard the word *treasure* a few times."

"Some people say good manners are a treasure. You shouldn't eavesdrop on private conversations."

The newcomer smiled at him coldly, and Brand noticed his right hand drop casually under the table.

"We can do this the easy way or the hard way. One way or another, you're going to tell me about the treasure. I just might want to have a look for it myself."

Brand decided things had gone far enough. It was obvious that the man had slipped a hidden knife from beneath his sleeve into his hand and was about to threaten him. He lashed out with his right foot and felt his heavy boot smash the man's hand against the bottom of the table. The knife clattered against the timber floor and the newcomer rocked out of his chair and staggered up.

In one motion Brand stood, kicked the blade out of reach, and sent his fist crashing into the man's stomach. It struck with a satisfying thud. The newcomer collapsed, winded and unable to speak.

"It's been a nice chat," Brand said, and walked out into the night.

The evening air was cold and he cursed himself. If he did not have such a smart mouth, and a tendency to violence, he would still be enjoying the warmth of the tavern and another drink. He should have spun a story for the scarred man and made him into a friend instead of an enemy. Always he was too quick to fight, and always he regretted it afterward, but he made the same mistake time and again.

A Gift

The next morning, when he called on the lòhren in his rooms at the palace, Aranloth opened the door and looked at him knowingly. His sea-gray eyes, as ever, absorbed everything but revealed nothing of himself.

He invited Brand in. "You've come to me with a purpose," he said, "and not merely to pass the time of day."

Brand's pulse quickened. "You've seen a vision?"

Aranloth chuckled. "I've seen no visions. But when a warrior knocks on the door of a lòhren with a frown on his face it means he wants advice. There's no magic in seeing that."

Brand told him of Felargin and the planned venture, and Aranloth listened attentively.

"Did he say why he picked you?"

"He told me he was looking for five of the best warriors in Cardoroth. He said I'd proven myself as such since my coming to the city."

Aranloth nodded. "Well, for someone who hasn't been here long you've earned a reputation. Trouble follows in your footsteps. You started as a wanderer, became a soldier and then a captain in the king's army almost overnight."

Brand grinned. "If trouble comes my way I won't back away from it. The king seems to like that."

Aranloth looked thoughtful before speaking again. "Did Felargin say why he wanted only five warriors?"

"He told me it would be enough to deal with any problems but not so many that the treasure would be spread too thin."

The lòhren grunted. "I don't suppose he told you how he knows where the treasure is?"

"He was vague. He only said that he thought something guarded it, but swore he knew exactly where it was. I don't trust him, but I'm sure he wasn't lying about that."

"I don't think so either," Aranloth said thoughtfully. "That's what worries me. Legends of the treasure have been circulating for decades. Everyone has heard the tale of Shurilgar the Sorcerer and the wealth he acquired by the betrayal of nations. Many have sought his lair near

Cardoroth, but nobody has ever found it. At least, nobody that returned to tell."

"You think there'll be danger, then?"

Aranloth raised an eyebrow. "You *know* it. You know also that Felargin doesn't intend to share the treasure and will try to kill you. Is the helm you seek, the heirloom of a long dead Duthenor chieftain, worth it?"

Brand answered without hesitation. "That chieftain was a relative of mine and came close to uniting all the tribes together. My people revere him and the immortal Halathrin gave the helm to him as a gift. They crafted it with unmatched skill and it's worth more than all other Duthenor treasures combined. With the helm on my head I could lead my tribe."

"You don't need the helm – you're the rightful chieftain by birth."

"Maybe so," Brand said quietly, "but with my parents killed and the chieftainship usurped, I need all the help I can get. You know I intend to reclaim it one day, but it won't be easy. The helm will aid me more than a crown."

"I won't try to persuade you against the venture. But though I haven't seen any visions, I think you'll encounter sorcery."

The lòhren gave him a gold ring. "This may help. If you're faced with magic, remove it from your finger."

Brand studied the ring, but it was unremarkable. "What use will it be if I take it *off*?"

"Just remember!" Aranloth said. "Things aren't always what they seem. You don't have to be a lòhren to understand that, do you?"

Brand spoke a little more with him, and then left his rooms. Aranloth wished him well when they parted, and he could see worry in his eyes, but he had a good feeling. The ring, whatever it could do, was on his finger, and he had a true-bladed sword by his side. Still, as he made his way along the cobbled streets, he could not help feeling a twinge of doubt. Felargin was not to be trusted, but what kind of trouble could such a weakling contrive?

The Quest Begins

The days passed without event and at the appointed time he rode from his barracks to Cardoroth's South Gate.

Felargin, looking like a scarecrow fashioned from sticks, waited on a placid chestnut mare and four warriors were with him. After quick introductions they passed through the gate and traveled south-west, Felargin in the lead. Brand considered them all as they rode.

The man known as Shorty spoke little. He was the smallest and wore a rapier. Rhaslin was a big man and hard muscles rippled beneath his red tunic. His weapon was a massive broadsword too heavy for most men to swing. Durnlak was sour-faced, dark-haired and of average build. His eyes, so brown as to be almost black, were smoldering pits and he looked like he had little use for other people. Bealegar was the last, a blond-haired and jovial sort who whistled as he rode and showed less sign than the others of nervousness.

Brand supposed they were all hiding fear. He knew he was. He was not only wary of what was to come, but also worried of adding to the danger by rash comments of his own. He was surrounded by strangers, each of them armed and of uncertain temperament.

The morning wore away and they rode toward the sweeping expanse of Lake Alithorin. Felargin led them along a path so faint that Brand doubted anyone would have found it without him.

The trail snaked back and forth, not seeming to head anywhere in particular, but it always took them deeper into tall stands of pine. It grew dark beneath them and the air was humid and filled with the smell of decomposition. Bright orange fungus flowered in lush growths on fallen trunks and lengths of gray-green moss trailed from overhead branches.

The travelers slowed down. Here, in the dark amid the trees, it felt like another world.

Shorty swayed to the left to avoid a low hanging trailer of moss. "This place gives me the shivers," he said.

Rhaslin laughed. "Are you scared of the woods, little man? Would you like to go back to Cardoroth and leave the treasure for the rest of us?"

"The wild holds no fears for me – but there's something different about this place," Shorty said.

"Woods are woods," answered Rhaslin. "And there's nothing in them that can't be killed by my blade."

Brand listened to their exchange but kept his opinion to himself; it would only cause an argument. There was something about Rhaslin that he did not like. He was too sure of himself and had dismissed Shorty's comment without thought. There *was* something unnerving about the woods.

Felargin led them on, and soon they headed uphill and away from the lake. Fog drifted from the water and cast groping fingers through the trees. Moisture clung in a film over the pine leaves and dripped from their needle-like ends. It was quiet and they saw no wildlife. There was only the distant howl of a lone wolf.

"How much further?" Durnlak asked.

Felargin did not slow his horse but turned in the saddle and grinned. "Soon."

Brand thought his smile even less warm than in the tavern. Their surroundings were disturbing, but nothing worried him as much as that.

The wolf howled again and Bealegar started. He looked at Brand and winked. "We'll get there when we get there," he said. "No point in getting worked up about things."

Brand nodded and the blond warrior whistled again, giving the impression he was merely strolling through Cardoroth's gardens.

Not long afterwards the trees thinned, and they faced rugged cliffs. The jagged overhang of the crags ensured the crannied surface ahead was shadowed. The path came to an end and the riders spread out around their now stationary guide.

Felargin raised a gaunt arm and pointed with a bony finger.

"I have led you truly. Behold! You see the resting place of treasures beyond your imagination. The wealth of kingdoms and the luster of gold lie within!"

Durnlak turned dark eyes on the man. "I see nothing but a wall of rock," he said bluntly.

Brand studied the cliff-face. Though he had not seen it before there *was* a cave there; the entrance little more than a man-sized shadow. The others now saw it too. He wondered how deep it went and what lay within.

Felargin dismounted and hitched his horse with a deft knot to a pine sapling. They all followed his lead.

A musty smell came from the entrance, but Brand could not place the odor. Was it the scent of some beast?

Rhaslin took a small lantern from his saddlebag and lit it. "Let's go. There's gold inside and little to fear." The warrior drew his massive broadsword and stepped forward.

Brand glanced at Felargin. He was smiling again; a visage no more appealing than the cave. He threw Shorty a look as they passed inside and read the same doubts on the little man's face. Treachery was afoot, and Shorty knew it too.

The Dust of Years

They moved into the cave and the light from the lantern cast swinging shadows but revealed little. Felargin, coming behind, produced his own lantern and their surroundings sprang into view.

The entrance was narrow but opened into a wide chamber with a sandy floor. Brand saw no tracks of man or beast, but the musty smell increased. The cave continued at a downward slope.

The travelers went down and the walls grew damp. Brand guessed they were going below the level of the lake. The floor soon gave way to a vast pit, and though its bottom was invisible, rubble formed a natural stairway. Rhaslin moved down on cat's feet and the others followed.

The floor at the bottom was of mud and ankle deep in water. When they disturbed it a putrid stench rose from the sludge.

Brand realized the walls were no longer natural but of chiseled stone. He did not doubt that the floor, had he been able to see it, was of flagstones. On the walls were the remnants of tapestries, long since rotted and spider-haunted. At some time in the past this room had been fashioned deep below the surface and later destroyed by earth tremors. Who had built it and why?

Bealegar gave a low whistle. "Look at *that*," the blond man said.

Brand followed his gaze and saw a series of statues in the dimness. They were the lifelike images of men and women, their features stern and aloof. The men had the look of arrogant warriors and the women were beautiful but remote.

Beyond the statues was a dais and upon it a throne. This was of black walnut and above the reach of the waters that periodically flooded the chamber. It was intact, the arms and legs embossed with scrollwork.

Rhaslin stepped past the throne to the wall behind it. "Is this it then?" He swung on Felargin. "Statues and rotted tapestries are your treasure?" He kicked the throne and the dust of years rose into the air.

Felargin was angry but swiftly regained his composure, for there was no trace of irritation when he spoke.

"Look at the wall," he said quietly. "It's not what it seems."

Rhaslin ripped the tapestry away. The stone was chipped and smudged. The big warrior looked at it blankly until Felargin moved beside him. He ran his thin-fingered hands like scuttling spiders across the surface and a hidden mechanism clicked.

"Push the wall," he said. Rhaslin placed his hands against it, and a doorway gave way at his touch.

The big warrior stepped through, holding his lantern high. Something within reflected the light. The others followed him, Brand and Shorty among them, spellbound by what they saw. The treasure of nations lay before them. Heaped carelessly across the floor were piles of gold and silver. Gems unnumbered winked the flickering light back at them. Weapons and armor hung on the walls, and Brand's gaze leapt to a silver helmet. The Helm of the Duthenor! All about them was wealth even greater than Felargin had promised.

Felargin! Where *was* he? Brand spun and noticed that Shorty was likewise moving to the door. Too late! It shut with a hollow boom.

Trial of Fear

"We're trapped!" yelled the little man.

"No need to worry," Rhaslin said. "We're sure to find a way to open it, and in the meantime the treasure is ours."

Brand's stomach churned. For what purpose had Felargin locked them in? He must know that eventually they would find, or force, a way out. Unless he did not think there would be time to do so...

He noticed now that scattered amongst the treasure were bones. Were they the remains of others that Felargin had led here? He glimpsed withered flesh and the moth-eaten remnants of clothing and shuddered.

"The smell is getting worse," Shorty said, and Brand knew that he was right. The air, which should have been still, was moving in slow eddies.

"The lantern is going out!" yelled Durnlak.

A chill gust blew across their faces, and grotesque shadows writhed over the treasure-strewn floor. With a hiss the light failed and darkness clutched them. They felt the primeval fear that had shadowed mankind since its rising from savagery to build fire and shelter against the night.

"We're in a tomb," whispered Durnlak.

Brand heard Rhaslin fumble to light the lantern but nothing worked. Then he sensed something in the chamber with them.

He felt a surge of panic as it whispered past him in the dark.

"Ahhhh," a cold and remote voice sighed. "I sense the warmth of flesh."

"Who speaks!" demanded Rhaslin.

The voice laughed, but there was no humor in the sound. It reminded Brand of Felargin's smile.

"Such arrogance. What meaning do names have? And yet once, when I walked the world of flesh, I had one."

"Shurilgar the Sorcerer," guessed Brand.

A moment later he cursed his rash words. It was foolish to draw attention to himself, for now he felt the weight of a vast intellect, steeped in arcane power, bear upon him.

"That *was* me. Now, I am a haunter of men's minds. Do you fear me?"

Brand clenched his teeth and did not answer.

The spirit's attention moved elsewhere. "Once I was a sorcerer and Felargin my apprentice. He serves me still. It's not easy for the dead to have power over the living, but there are ways. He brings me offerings, and in return I teach him secrets that would burn other minds. After your deaths, I'll reveal to him yet more. He awaits outside."

"How do you intend to kill us? You're only a spirit," scoffed Rhaslin. "What power do you have over the living?"

"What power? Shall I show you powers undreamed of? Shall I show you the truth even as death rends the flesh from your bones?"

Brand's heart skipped a beat as he heard the slow pad of feet. He tried to step back but could not move a muscle. Desperately he struggled to reach for his sword, but his body would not respond.

The padding moved on and a growl, slow and menacing, filled the chamber.

Durnlak screamed. Slavering jaws and moans of agony rent the air. The stench of an opened abdomen filled the chamber. Durnlak's moaning grew low and pitiful before ceasing. The warrior was dead, but the ghost-beast had not finished. There was a sharp crack as it split bone between its jaws.

Who would be next? Brand gave up reaching for his sword. It would be easier to move a mountain than shift his arm a few inches. He remembered Aranloth's gift and struggled in vain to flex his thumb, to push it against the ring on his finger and remove it as Aranloth advised. Sweat broke out on his brow, but he could not do it.

The padding sounded once more and the smell of dust rose from the floor. The beast stood before him. He felt its warm breath against his legs and the hair on the back of his neck rose, but the creature moved away.

The voice of Rhaslin broke the silence. "*Please*. Take the others. I'll serve you!" But there was no answer to his pleading. The big warrior sobbed. There was a ripping sound and he screamed, a high-pitched wail that surely carried through the door to Felargin. The big warrior moaned. "Help me," he begged.

But nobody could so much as turn their heads in his direction. Brand at last gained the slightest movement of his thumb and it twitched a hair's breadth against the ring. Yet there was so much further to go and so little time. Rhaslin's cries were now weak. The warrior who appeared to fear nothing turned out to be a coward. Maybe such a death would make cowards of them all.

The dreaded padding began again. The creature stopped near Shorty and a deep growl rumbled in its throat. The little man made no noise and the creature moved on. Bealegar yelled. His voice rent the air in defiance.

Brand strove madly against the unnatural force holding him. The ring moved on his finger, bit by bit, but even if he freed it what could it achieve?

Bealegar groaned and the sound of the ghost-beast's muffled breathing came to the others. It was snuffling, its snout buried deep in flesh.

At length there was a rattle, the last breath of the blond warrior as he died in near silence. Would the ghost-beast come for him or Shorty? Desperately, Brand continued to twitch his thumb against the ring.

The padding drew toward him. He felt the hot breath of the creature's snout against his legs. Then it reared up, the claws of its heavy paws scratching his chest. Saliva dribbled on his neck, and the fetid stench of rank breath blew over his face. His instinct was to struggle and draw his sword, but he ignored that and continued twitching his thumb.

The creature's weight dropped from him and it moved toward Shorty. The little warrior laughed and the padding stopped. It seemed that Shorty was a bigger man than he looked, and Brand distantly sensed the weight of the ghost-beast's vast intellect concentrate upon his companion.

Suddenly Brand's thumb twitched strongly and the ring fell. It hit the floor with a sound like a small bell but spun like a dropped coin.

The creature gave an uncertain growl. The bell-like sound of the ring increased, and now there was faint light. It grew quickly and revealed once more the treasure-strewn floor. The ghost-beast vented a howl that turned Brand's blood cold but was not in sight.

A bright light spun up all around them, and Brand could see the ring was no more. In its place was a disk of light spinning quicker than the eye could follow, though it was already beginning to fade.

"I can move!" Shorty said. Brand whipped his head around and scanned the chamber, but there was no sign of the creature anywhere.

He looked at his companions who lay on the floor. They were dead, of that there was no doubt. And yet there were no marks upon their bodies; no blood or wounds. Maybe Rhaslin had been right after all: the dead had no power over the living. Was it possible though that Shurilgar had killed them by the power of suggestion alone?

He scooped up the Helm of the Duthenor. Placing it on his head he drew his sword. Shorty snatched a handful of gold coins, and together they ran to the door.

"Any ideas?" asked Shorty.

Brand shook his head and studied the stone. "I can't see anything, but I'd guess it can be opened from this side."

He ran his hands along the stone. Perhaps the mechanism could only be felt and not seen? The light flared brightly for a moment then suddenly died.

It was pitch dark again and Brand felt dread encroach on his soul. The ghost-beast howled; a sound of pure hatred. He felt something give and the door sprang open. The two men leaped through. Felargin was there and scrambled to his feet leaving his lit lantern on the floor. He raised his arms, but whatever spell he was preparing to cast Brand was quicker. He knew now that he was a sorcerer and was taking no chances. His fist cracked into the traitor's chin and Felargin stumbled but righted himself straight away. He was tougher than he looked!

Shorty, who was free to run if he chose, instead drew his rapier and slashed at Felargin, but the sorcerer stepped nimbly aside and snapped a lightning kick at the little man's head that knocked him down. Felargin raised his arms once more, but Brand was ready. He did not punch but shoulder-charged him. This was something Felargin had not expected and it sent him flying through the open door.

Brand pulled it closed and heard a rush of padded feet. The door slammed and he felt a thud as something crashed into it from the other side.

There was a muted scream. The ghost-beast had been deprived of its prey, but nothing would stay its hatred now. There was a noise that might have been sobbing and then silence.

Shorty was pale as death, though he spoke with conviction. "Only what he deserved." The little man was unsteady on his feet, and blood streamed from his nose.

Brand nodded. "I underestimated him badly." He adjusted the helm on his head.

"That suits you," Shorty said.

"We both got something for our troubles – but it's time to leave."

The cavern seemed calm and peaceful now, but he had learned not to rely on appearances. Was the ghost-beast restricted to the treasure-chamber, or could it roam free?

Daylight and Danger

"Let's go," agreed Shorty.

Brand walked side by side with the little man and felt good. Not only had he found the Helm of the Duthenor, but a friend as well.

They came out of the darkness into bright light. The joy they should have felt at surviving died in their hearts though. Four men waited near the cave entrance: silent, blades drawn and murder in their cold glance.

58

The scarred man from the tavern was their leader, and Brand cursed himself. He could have avoided this. He made certain his hand was far from his sword's hilt and attempted to talk his way out of the situation.

"You've followed us for nothing, I'm afraid." He opened up his hands and held them out. "As you can see, we salvaged nothing from the venture."

"You'd sure like us to believe that," the scarred man said. "But you're wearing a fancy helm now, and the runt beside you might have handfuls of gems in his pockets."

Shorty raised his eyebrows. "Name-calling is for the handsome, son. With a face like a bucket of fish guts, you should learn to keep quiet."

Brand gritted his teeth. There would be a fight now, and men would die. He searched for words to break the tension, but before he spoke a howl tortured the air, and a stench drifted from the cave entrance.

The scarred man's helpers looked at each other with pale faces. "What on earth is that?" asked one of them.

Brand thought quickly. "Death for us all unless we ride!"

He took a gamble and ran for his horse. He made no motion to draw his sword and sped right past the men as though he was more afraid of what was in the cave. The men saw this, and convinced by his actions more than his words, ran for their own horses.

Shorty was right behind him, fear on his face once more. The scarred man led his men on a wild gallop into the dim forest. Brand hesitated a moment, and then went toward the lake and the bright light near its open shore.

He turned to his companion when they got there. "You could've got us killed, you know."

Shorty shrugged. "Felargin might have fooled me. But I still know fish guts when I see them."

4. The Forgotten Queen

A whisper. A murmur in the dark. A brush of strange thoughts that were not his own.

Brand glanced at Taingern's freckled face as they tramped the narrow streets of Cardoroth City. Most revelers had long since found their beds. His friend hummed a soldier's song and concentrated only on putting one foot in front of the other.

It was the wrong side of midnight, the wrong side of another birthday, and Brand's mood was melancholy.

Hear me! Hear me!

His hair shivered upright and his skin prickled.

Was he drunk? He had spent enough coin in the tavern to make a homesick mariner raise both eyebrows. Yet his senses remained sharp.

He kept going. The whole night had seemed odd, and he could not shake the feeling that the years of his life flowed like water through his grasping fingers. He wanted to be more than a captain in the army. He yearned to achieve something special, to leave a mark on Cardoroth, even if it was not his home city. *Especially* because it was not his home city. He wanted the world to remember him long after his last birthday was celebrated.

Come! Defend your queen!

This time even Taingern heard it. "What in blazes was that?"

Brand unsheathed his sword. "Where's it coming from?"

They stood back to back, weapons drawn, but the narrow street was empty. Buildings rose tall and dark on either side. Crows, somehow disturbed from their roosts, cried sharply. Starlight flickered to their wing beats. Ahead, the lane curved around a shadow-haunted park. A strange light flared above the treetops.

Brand pointed with his sword. "There!"

Taingern turned and watched. His face, freckled and honest, shone palely in the dim light.

"The Tower of Halathgar," he said hoarsely.

"What's that?" asked Brand.

Taingern looked at him with wide eyes. "You've never heard of the Witch Queen's tower?"

"I've seen it often enough, but I've never heard that name before."

"Well, it's one of those things. Everybody knows it's there. Most hear rumors – but few know much. I guarded it several years ago."

"Why does it need guarding?"

Taingern shivered. "The general never told us. But the story we had from an old soldier was that her crypt lies under the foundations. He swore it was filled with ancient treasure."

The crows flapped madly overhead. Their eerie nighttime cawing was redoubled by the stone sides of the buildings.

Come! Defend your queen. I command you!

Brand's vision blurred. His stomach churned, and suddenly he looked out as though from a great height. A cold wind buffeted his face. His vision cleared. The city of Cardoroth, all its tall buildings, its cobbled streets, its squares, markets and many-fountained parks, glinted in the light of an infinity of stars. A constellation of two brilliant points hung directly above. They burned in the night sky like eyes boring into the stone pinnacle of the tower, on which he somehow stood.

61

With a wrench he looked up from the street once more. "Let's go!"

The two of them raced along the cobbled lane and into the park. Blackness lay in drifts beneath the trees like the leaf-fall of a thousand shadowy nights.

The Tower of Halathgar stood just ahead, a great structure of red marble, round and tapered to a high, crenellated summit.

Taingern drew to a sudden halt.

"What is it?" asked Brand.

"There aren't any guards."

"So?"

"There are *always* guards. Night and day."

Brand studied the tower door by the flickering light of two torches that burned in brackets to either side. It was of weathered oak. The brass doorknob, cast as a wolf's head and smoothed by centuries of use, was set above a lock deeply recessed into the ancient wood.

He pointed. "Look at that."

The lock was twisted and ruined, the timber encasing the metal blasted by fire.

He put his weight against the door and shoved. It groaned and opened. Taking one of the torches, he led the way into the dark mouth of the tower.

The Tower of the Witch Queen

They found the guards inside. Two of them. Their corpses lay in a tangle of out-flung limbs and broken bones at the base of the spiral staircase that wound to the top. Scorch marks blackened their clothes, and blood seeped onto the cold stone. Beside them, a heavy trap door led to the basement.

Brand did not recognize them. But they wore the same uniform that he did, had sworn the same oath to serve and protect Cardoroth. They deserved a better end.

"Why are they burned?" he asked.

Taingern peered at them for a moment. "I don't know."

"Then let's find out."

His companion shook his head. "I think we should summon help. These two men were outmatched – and we are only two ourselves."

Brand did not pause. "Whoever murdered these soldiers might get away if we don't catch them now. Besides, the crows are making enough noise to alert even tomorrow's City Guard."

Taingern frowned. "You're mad," he muttered. "But I'll not have it said that I turned my back and ran."

Brand started up the stairs.

"Wait," Taingern said. "If that was the Witch Queen's voice we heard, her crypt will be down below."

"Probably," agreed Brand. "But whatever's happening is going on up the top." There was no time to explain his vision. "I know it."

He raced up the stairwell. It circled inside the tower wall and they passed a series of locked doors that led to inner rooms. They reached the ninth floor and found another two guards, dead like the first. The door that opened onto the top of the tower stood ajar. There was a sound of stone grinding against stone, which culminated in something heavy dropping. A boom reverberated throughout the tower, and shudders ran beneath their feet.

Brand rested his torch against the wall and inched toward the opening. He saw only a narrow view of an open platform and a sliver of the star-laden sky. Stepping forward on soft feet, he edged through the gap. Taingern followed closely, and together they crept onto the tower summit.

A chill wind blew into their faces. The city stretched out below. It lay like a blanket of shadows, disturbed by the occasional light in a window or by torches in well-frequented streets.

In the center of the platform a stone monument rose knee-high from the floor. Brand stalked toward it. The structure's sides were great slabs of red marble, engraved with strange script and sculpted in high relief with scenes of battle. Carrion crows circled above contending armies and wolves prowled the horizon. The single slab that served as a lid was thrown down beside it. One edge, crumbled and scorched by fire, faced toward him.

A black-robed man in high boots stood beside the monument. He leaned close to look inside. The metal brooch on his cloak gleamed, and there was a sheen of starlight on the supple wych-wood staff that he carried. A deep cowl obscured his face, but his hands, one gripping the staff, the other on the edge of the monument, were pallid and blue-veined. He was still. Only his head moved, turning and pivoting in slow study of whatever lay inside.

A sorcerer! Brand felt a wave of fear drive away the last effects of the night's drinking. He halted, but the figure must have already sensed his presence. The head rotated toward him, and he felt the pressure of a chill gaze from the shadowed face.

Ancient Enmity

There was a moment of shock before the sorcerer hissed like a squall of storm-driven rain. He leaned forward and scrutinized Brand. The pallid skin of his face became visible. His eyes remained hidden.

64

Brand could not decide whether to attack or flee. Even as a foreigner he knew that sorcerers held a vendetta against Cardoroth. They were sworn to destroy it, and he should fight. But dread of their unnatural powers held him fixed to the spot.

After several moments, the sorcerer stepped from the monument and raised his staff. A stream of fire flared from its tip and sizzled through the air.

The impelling fear of death launched Brand and Taingern into sudden motion and they leaped and rolled. They avoided the searing flame that lit the top of the tower like a beacon and raced toward the black-robed man.

Swift as a lurching shadow the sorcerer dodged. Once more flame burst from the wych-wood staff. Brand was not quick enough this time; a tongue of fire licked at his boots and he stumbled and fell.

Gnawing heat bit through leather and he surged upright as Taingern slashed at their opponent. The sharp-edged blade cut the air in front of the man's neck but he responded with a flurry of robes and kicked Taingern in the chest.

Brand winced as he saw the dark figure's iron-shod boot smash into his friend. The heel was a drùgluck sign: three slanted lines within a circle. The symbol of ill omen that sorcerers used as their mark.

Taingern sprawled to the floor near the monument. The sorcerer raised his staff, red flame burning at its tip, but before he could bring it to bear Brand attacked. He drove the point of his sword forward, but once again his opponent was too quick. The sorcerer deflected the thrusting blade with his staff and then whipped the supple wood across Brand's knuckles. The blow knocked the sword from his grip. It clattered against the stone flagging and the black figure rushed him.

Brand managed to wrench the staff from him as they tussled but then cold hands, hard as iron, seized his throat and the sorcerer forced him back against the crenellated balustrade of the tower. He struggled, but the man's power was raw and brutal. Brand could not breathe.

The sorcerer stared, his face now visible, pallid and blue-veined like his hands. Dark circles rimmed the bottom of his fevered eyes.

"You will die tonight," he said. "Know this, though. Had you not interfered you would have died soon anyway. The long years have not slaked my brethren's hatred for your city and all within it. Tonight, we shall rejoice, for the prophesied death of your king will come to pass, and the means of the city's destruction will be in our hands."

The death-grip about Brand's throat tightened and he grew dizzy. Through a haze he saw Taingern come to his feet on shaky legs, raise his sword and stumble toward them.

The sorcerer must have heard his approach and turned his head to look. Brand guessed what would happen next. His attacker would swing him around, fling him against Taingern, and retrieve his staff.

Brand bunched his knees in readiness for his last chance. When the sorcerer started to move, he drove up with all his strength and with the certainty that if they could not kill their enemy now, he would be free to work whatever evil he intended.

His frantic effort caught the man by surprise. He lifted the sorcerer off the floor, tried to heave him over the ledge, but he weighed too much. Brand's legs buckled, but at that moment Taingern drove his sword into their enemy's side and pushed. Their opponent hissed. Black robes flared and rippled as he plunged over the edge of the tower, the sword fixed in his side. There was a sickening thump, and the crows in the park flapped and cawed.

Brand heaved for breath and drank deeply of the cold, sweet air.

Taingern tenderly felt his chest, and a grimace contorted his freckled face. "Well, it nearly got us killed, but at least we found out what was happening up here."

Brand managed a smile. "Not quite," he said. "We still don't know what the sorcerer was trying to do."

Nothing Lasts Forever

He retrieved his sword from the stone-flagged floor. Sheathing the blade, he hesitated only a moment before continuing toward the monument. Whatever the sorcerer had wanted was in that box-like structure. And he had gone to a great deal of trouble to get it.

Taingern muttered behind him like a cranky old man, but Brand knew that his companion felt the same sense of curiosity. Otherwise, he would never have dared to come up to the top of the tower.

"I'll flip you for it," Brand said.

"Flip me for what?"

"For which of us gets to look inside first."

Taingern swore under his breath.

"Don't say I didn't offer," Brand said.

He stepped closer to the monument. The wind eased and the crows grew silent. Stars glittered overhead with a cold light. He leaned over the stone edge and gazed within. Taingern stood right next to him.

At the bottom were bones, broken and fragmented. The flesh of a body, laid to rest in antiquity, had decayed to dust. The skull, white and stark, glared back at them; under its dislodged jaw rested a torc, its twisted gold filmed by ancient grime. Jewels, rings, coins and other treasures of a past age glinted in the dull light.

"The Witch Queen," whispered Taingern. "She's not buried in the basement after all."

Brand did not answer. Even as his companion spoke, the crows in the park clamored madly, and the cold wind stirred to life once more. The dust at the bottom of the sarcophagus, that once had formed flesh and blood, seethed. An ethereal shape rose in a swirl of color and they staggered back.

The image of a woman stood tall and majestic before them. She gazed down at the two men, her eyes terrible and stern. They were blue, cold as Lake Alithorin in winter, but her skin was ruddy, and her unbound hair shone like spilled blood. Luxurious curls ran down her long back and shimmered in the frigid air. She was a massive figure, heavy-boned and thick-limbed. The gold torc they had seen in the sarcophagus gleamed brilliantly about her neck, and her body was clothed in a tunic of many colors. In her right hand she grasped an iron-headed spear as though ready to strike.

Her stare bored into them. "I called for help, and this is all that come? Two men out of an entire city."

They gave no answer and her eyes narrowed. "Do you even know who I am?"

Brand had no intention of voicing the term *Witch Queen*. He did not know what powers she had or what her purposes were. He feared to find out.

"You were once a queen of this realm," he said.

She turned her gaze upon him and he shivered.

"How swiftly the centuries forget!" Her fingers wrapped around the spear shaft with great force. "Some called me the Battle Queen. Some Carnhaina. But my enemies knew me as Halathgar, for I was born under the light of those two stars, the constellation of the Lost

Huntress. My enemy's prophets foretold I would destroy them – and so I did! Those stars watched over my birth, my long reign, and even in death they shine upon me."

She looked up at the two bright points, and their light glittered in her eyes and sparked off the iron edges of the spear tip.

Brand took a deep breath. "What did the sorcerer want?"

She gnashed her teeth. "What do all sorcerers want? Power!"

She laughed then, and he was not sure if she was altogether sane.

"And I have power! Yes, even in death. He would have stolen something, an heirloom that was ancient before I was born, old before my father founded Cardoroth. It was forged in the forgotten deeps of time, ere our race established mighty realms, when they still worshipped around rings of standing stones and celebrated the sun's birth each year. If the sorcerer had his way, he would reduce us to that again, or worse, for he descends from the enemies I once defeated."

She looked at them in turn with her stern eyes. "But you thwarted him and have your queen's gratitude. I shall reward you."

Brand was uneasy. What would a long-dead queen consider a suitable reward?

"It's enough that we served the city," he said.

"Ha!" she barked. "You did more than serve it. You saved it – for a while."

She swept a hand through the air and rings glittered on each of her fingers.

"Look! Watch our beloved Cardoroth."

They stepped away from the sarcophagus and stared out over the battlements. What they beheld was a vision of destruction. Brand saw that the West Gate was fallen, the metal ruined and broken. The guard tower, thrown down into a rubble of bricks and broken bodies, no longer blocked the way. Cardoroth's enemies poured into her and the city burned. Smoke roiled in black plumes from the windows of stone buildings, and red flame leaped and danced wherever there was timber. People ran madly through the streets: the rich, the poor, the young and the old, the high and the low. They trampled each other in panic, and the enemy pursued them, swords wetted by blood.

The palace ran with gore as the last defense faltered before a rising wave of enemies. Screams of fear, cries of terror, and shouts of mad glee rose up to the pinnacle of the tower.

Brand shuddered. Would he and Taingern live to see this? Or would it happen when they were dust like the Witch Queen? Either way, it pierced his heart.

He turned to her. "Enough!" he said.

She waved her hand through the air once more. "So will Cardoroth end."

The queen's eyes glimmered, and a change came over her voice. She spoke quietly, almost as if the two men no longer stood before her.

"Nothing lasts forever. Not people. Not queens. Not even cities…"

Brand stood in silent thought, and the queen studied him with watchful eyes.

"Have you learned something, Captain?"

"Yes," Brand said. "We all perish – but that's not worth a puff of smoke. What counts is how we get there."

The Witch Queen regarded him with a strange look. At length she spoke again.

"Know this. Neither the evil that men do, nor suffering and hardship, endures either. All things pass.

70

The bad as well as the good. Think of my words whenever you are sorely tried."

The queen hesitated. "In remembrance of me, will you take this gift?"

She removed a silver band from her finger, a signet ring, with a flat emerald set on top. Carved on the face of the stone was an image of the Tower of Halathgar. Two diamonds, like the twin stars of the Lost Huntress, glinted above it.

Brand accepted the ring from her cold hands, and then she reached into the dust at the bottom of her sarcophagus and scooped a great handful of gold coins. These she handed to Taingern.

She regarded them both. "In life, I only took. If I gave more, maybe I would be better remembered."

She lowered the spear and closed her eyes. The motes of dust that formed her figure drifted apart and settled to the base of the sarcophagus.

"I hear you, Carnhaina," Brand said.

5. The Choice

Brand gazed through the slit-like window of his small office. He hoped the view would offer relief from his troubles. Instead, it deepened them.

He traced the length of the white road that scarred the chalky soil around Cardoroth city. It cut a line to the West Gate, a long way below his cramped room in the guard tower. He had ridden that dusty path many times; attacking armies had marched its length more often still.

The litter of sieges lay abandoned in the pastures to either side. Long grass grew green where seeking roots reached deep into the soil. Legions of enemy dead rested there, but their living brethren outnumbered them.

He caught a glimmer of light on far-off Lake Alithorin. His gaze lingered before he surveyed the shadow-laden pinewoods that rimmed its shores. He knew those nighted haunts. He had explored the misty tree-aisles and even learned some of the forest's deadly secrets.

Danger did not worry him. At least not much. He liked the feel of a sword hilt in his hand. It was better than the quill he now used so often; better than signing rosters, tallying equipment or the requisitioning of supplies and settling of disputes between soldiers that occupied so much of his time. The view of the outside world, the world that once he roamed freely, only served to remind him of how bored he was as a captain in the army.

An urgent knock at the door distracted him. What new administrative torture would this be?

"Enter!" He regretted the abruptness of his tone. The soldier who came into the room, just old enough to shave, nervously slammed a fist into his chest by way of salute.

Brand casually opened his left palm in the customary acknowledgement, and offered a smile.

"At ease, soldier."

The youth still looked tense.

"Thank you, Sir."

Brand deliberately slouched in his chair. Adopting a casual posture encouraged the men he supervised to relax.

"What can I do for you?"

The soldier cleared his throat. "Someone wants to see you."

Brand waited patiently. When no further information came, he raised an eyebrow as encouragement.

"It's the old lady, Sir."

"And what old lady is that?"

"Sorry Sir. I forget sometimes that you're not from Cardoroth. I mean *the* old lady. She's lived on a farm just out from the gate for as long as anyone in this part of the city remembers. She sells cheese every day at the markets."

Brand sighed. "Her cheese must be good if she's been selling it that long. Why does she want to see me, though?"

"Yes Sir. Sorry Sir. She's also a seer."

Brand leaned forward with sudden interest. He believed in seers, at least some of them. Several had sought him out over the years – they told him that he cast a shadow in the otherworld, whatever that meant.

"What does she want, son?"

The soldier shrugged. "She wouldn't say. She just demanded to see you ... and she usually gets her way."

Brand stood up. "Then I won't disappoint her."

The Choice

They found her by the gate. It was open, its massive bars nicked and scored by the enemy's frequent attacks. She leaned against an ancient handcart filled with wax-coated cheeses. Two guards stood next to her under the shadow of the missile-pocked wall. They laughed good-naturedly at something she said but snapped to attention when they saw Brand.

The old lady studied him carefully. "You're Brand?"

He nodded. "How may I help you, madam?"

Her nut-brown face crinkled in what might have been a smile.

"You have good manners – for a wild man from the lands of the Duthenor."

"If you're a seer, lady, you will know that I'm more than a wild man."

"Ha! I know your past. But that's of no matter now. It's the future that interests me."

"What of it?" asked Brand.

She studied him. Her threadbare shawl, older even than the cart, was taut over her shoulders and her short coarse hair. The sun-beaten skin of her brow furrowed and her jaw wriggled as she thought.

"Are you loyal to Cardoroth?" she asked suddenly. Her eyes, the outer portion yellow and the inner cloudy, peered at him questioningly.

Brand inclined his head. "A fair question, lady. There's nothing I wouldn't do for Cardoroth. But were I not loyal ... still might I answer so."

She laughed loudly but held her rheumy eyes upon him.

74

"Thus do you rebuke me for my impertinence. Yet it was a courteous rebuke."

Brand made no reply.

The old lady cackled. "Now you wish to encourage me to get on and speak my piece. Very well!"

A change came over her. She straightened and held her head high. Her eyes sharpened upon him and there was sudden clarity in her gaze. She looked like a hawk that rode the high airs before it plummeted to seize its prey.

"Cardoroth stands in peril," she said. "Not yet of armies, nor of the numberless enemies without her walls who plot to bring her down. This enemy is within. One of our own will betray us – I have seen it."

She paused. Her jaw trembled and threads of once-black hair escaped her shawl and fluttered in the breeze.

"Speak on," Brand said.

"You will meet him before three days are done. And when you do, you must make a choice."

"What choice, lady?"

She tilted her head to study him better. "The choice of life or death."

Brand took a step back from her fierce gaze. "What does that mean?"

"It means that you will have the power to save him. Others will try to kill him. You can offer protection, and condemn the city to destruction, or walk away, and let fate take its course. It's his life, or the city."

Brand studied her closely. "And why tell me?"

The old lady shrugged. She seemed to shrink and her eyes appeared rheumy once more.

"It's part of my burden. I must speak what I see."

"And what of the man. Have you spoken to him, too?"

She slid her fingers along the tattered edge of her shawl and tucked in the stray tendrils of hair. The skin on the back of her hand was wrinkled like sun-dried clay at the bottom of a long-emptied pond.

"Oh yes – I've seen him. He told me to mind my own business. He'll be a fool to the end, that one. I don't need the sight to see that."

"And what do you expect me to do?"

The old lady shrugged. "I expect nothing. I saw a vision and spoke it – what will be will be. There's no use fighting it."

She took up the handles of her cart and mumbled to herself as she stomped away.

Brand slept poorly that night. It was not in his nature to let a group fight and kill a lone man. Yet he was loyal to Cardoroth, and the life of a single person, especially a traitor, was a small thing compared to the lives of the multitude.

For Cardoroth

He rose early. If he could not sleep, he would try to clear his mind before he faced the slow barrage of boredom that waited in his office.

He wandered through the lonely streets of the city. A crimson dawn shot rays of light over the tile rooftops and brushed the red marble of the higher walls. The scent of new-baked bread ran like a river down the shadowed streets. He bought a small loaf. It steamed in the cold air when he broke it.

He passed the Hamalath, the open-air theater where he had watched plays performed and learned much of the history of the city. He also passed the Merenloth, where philosophers debated and bards chanted ancient lays. Thousands of stone seats, terraced in curved rows into the slope, overlooked the small stage. The stands, though empty now, often filled with listening crowds. Cardoroth was like no place he had ever been before; it was a combination of ancient mysteries, wisdom, life, laughter and friendship. He imagined it sacked by the enemy, its streets reddened by blood and screams rending the air. He would not have that on his conscience.

People began to move about, and the streets filled with crowds. He entered a park to avoid them. He was not born in the city, but he had learned to love it. It was proud, even noble. It deserved its place in the sun and he would not jeopardize it.

He wandered to a beech tree surrounded by short grass. The trunk, gray and smooth, ascended gracefully to the sky. Stately boughs spread in a mighty canopy and dappled sunlight settled to the earth like green-gold dew. He leaned against the trunk, closed his eyes and tried to make peace with his decision.

The leaves of the beech whispered and sighed. The rich scent of the earth, deep beneath his boots, swelled in the air. Somewhere in the distance, a thick-beaked nudaluk bird hammered away at a tree trunk in search of insects.

Brand remained still and sought oneness with the morning. He did not find it. The swift noise of galloping horses distracted him and his eyes flicked open. Four riders streaked across the park. A fine chestnut mare led and the others strained to catch up. Their hooves threw up a spray of clods that scattered and fell long after they passed.

Suddenly the rider of the chestnut mare changed direction. The horse now angled toward the beech tree. It sucked in great gulps of air and sweat foamed over its flanks. It sped over the grass, each blade crusted by a sheath of frost.

The rider came beneath the eaves of the tree and tried to change direction again. This time the weary horse slipped. It crashed to the ground, and its flank scraped a long gouge in the earth. The dislodged rider, a youth verging on manhood, landed heavily beneath the tree canopy.

Brand watched as the three pursuing riders pulled up their mounts and leaped off. The moment the seer warned of had arrived. It was still unexpected and he was not ready. But what else did he need to know? The youth would betray Cardoroth.

The pursuers drew their swords and walked toward the youth. He whimpered in pain as he stood, and then tried to hobble to his horse. One of the men, only a little older, kicked him to the ground.

Brand trembled as he watched. This was no vision playing out before him, no dry telling of a person's fate: it was real life and soon bright blood would stain the silver-frosted grass.

He stepped away from the trunk, and the three men noticed him. They wheeled in his direction.

A black-haired man with a pale scar on his cheek stepped forward.

"What're you looking at?"

Brand had met his kind before. Any hint of weakness would draw an attack from the scarred man, and the other two would follow his lead. They were all in the mood for trouble, and he must either walk away or try to out-bluff their leader.

He made his choice. "Not the pride of Cardoroth, obviously. Three against one? Is that how you measure yourselves as men?"

The black-haired man reddened, and his scar shone white. "He cheated us at cards. And not for the first time. He won't get the chance to do it again."

"You would kill someone for that? It seems you're just as much to blame for being stupid enough to play cards with him more than once."

Scarface raised his sword. His mouth twisted and his eyes flared with rabid light. Brand realized that he had made a mistake. Bluffing did not work with crazy people. The man's companions edged closer behind their leader, but Brand sensed their reluctance.

He forced himself to look relaxed and calm. "Why don't you ride away now – before any harm is done."

Scarface hawked and spat. His hand tightened on the hilt of his short sword, and his shoulder lifted slightly. Brand read the signs of imminent attack and nearly drew his own sword. Instead, he took a great risk. He rocked his weight onto his back leg as the black-haired man's blade cut through the cold air. At the same time, his front leg kicked swift and hard into his opponent's groin.

Scarface screamed and rolled onto the ground. The sword dropped from his hand to lie still on the frosted grass while its owner writhed.

Brand looked at the man's two companions. His heart thumped. It would have been safer to have drawn his weapon and killed. He allowed none of his fear to show though. He now rested his hand on his sword hilt to emphasize the words he spoke next.

"Take your friend away. I'm done playing – I'll kill the next person who attacks me."

The two men fumbled to sheath their swords and then helped their comrade onto his horse. He began to vomit, but they held him from falling as they rode off.

Brand went to help the youth up. "What's your name, son."

"Balhain. And I don't need your help."

The youth limped over to his horse and took the reins. It heaved for breath and steamed in the cold.

Brand gazed after him in amazement. "Really? If you felt that way why didn't you say something while your friends were here?"

The youth mounted, looked at him with a surly expression, and spat.

"They're not my friends – and neither are you."

He kicked the horse into a canter and rode away without another word.

Brand cursed. Loudly and in detail. He had put Cardoroth in jeopardy for this? He took some calming breaths. That was not the point. If the youth betrayed the city, it would be something that he would have to live with. Brand, for his part, could not live with allowing a group to attack and kill a single man. No matter the circumstances. And Cardoroth would not be worth saving if its people condoned such a thing.

He strode toward the West Gate. Maybe another day of boredom was not as bad as he thought. At least it was predictable. Anyway, his mind, and his conscience, were clear.

He came to the tower entrance and the old lady was there, waiting for him. She leaned against her cart and looked at him knowingly.

"You allowed him to live?"

Brand shrugged. "I won't condemn a man for an act that he *might* commit."

"Then you have condemned Cardoroth."

"Maybe. But no fate is certain. The future is nothing more than the flicker of shadows, no matter what story a seer reads into them. It can loom first one way, then another, just as firelight reaches up, then subsides. Who among us, seer or otherwise, can see the true path that a man will walk among all his choices?"

The old lady stared at him long and hard. At length she inclined her head. "What you say is true. But know this – Balhain was not the one of whom I spoke. In my vision, the scar-faced man betrayed us. His name is Gildar."

Brand was momentarily startled, and then he laughed. He nearly *had* killed him.

6. I Choose Death

The remembered death rattle of a thousand throats rang in Brand's ears.

He shivered despite the hot sunlight and tried to shake off the soul-sapping fatigue of battle. The enemy, repelled many times during the morning, regrouped for yet another attack. He closed his eyes, but that only sharpened his recollection of the crash of sword on helm, the shouting of doomed soldiers, the cries of hatred and screams of pain; the begging for help while men writhed on the blood-streaked grass or sat wide-eyed and unnaturally still, their spilled bowels cradled in pale hands. He forced his eyes open.

King Gilhain commanded the army from the crest of a rise. His silver helm, burnished to a faultless gleam, sparked like leaping fire. The royal banner fluttered at the touch of an intermittent breeze, and his personal guard of thirty men, the famed Durlin, ringed him. Their chainmail glittered and the white surcoats they wore with legendary pride blazed under the noontide sun. It was not Brand's first battle though, and neither the sight of his much-loved king, nor the renowned guard, stirred him. He looked away. *The actions of the humble are more impressive than the show of the illustrious.*

Just as it had all morning, the unnerving chant of the enemy swelled through the air.

Ashrak ghùl skar! Skee ghùl ashrak!
Skee ghùl ashrak! Ashrak ghùl skar!

He knew what it meant. So did all the citizens of Cardoroth City. Everyone learned those words in childhood – and feared them. They formed the battle cry of the elug nation.

Death and destruction! Blood and death!
Blood and death! Death and destruction!

Brand's gaze drifted to Arawdan, the Durlindrath who led the Durlin. In that group of thirty men, the pride of the whole country was embodied. Each had sworn an unbreakable oath to protect the king. He was a brilliant strategist, and except for him, the enemy would long ago have plundered Cardoroth. The Durlin had defied sword, knife and assassin's poison to keep the king alive. While he survived, Cardoroth endured. And that made him the target of innumerable attacks. It was only a matter of time before one of them was successful, but that never stopped the Durlin, and Brand knew it would never stop him, either.

A redheaded youth next to Brand followed his gaze.

"Is it true that Arawdan is covered in scars?"

Brand thought about it.

"He's got his fair share. I was there when he collected the last. He took an arrow in the back that was intended for the king."

The youth looked suitably impressed, though Brand doubted he had enough experience to appreciate the situation. Talk was easy, but few had the willpower and steadiness of mind to guard the king for weeks, months and years, wondering all the while when an attack would come. It was no way to live, yet Arawdan somehow stayed affable.

The youth gestured at the elugs with a freckled hand. "What's going to happen next?"

Brand looked over the trampled grass, beyond the grotesque bodies of the slain, to the enemy.

"Keep your eyes on the *shazrahad*," he said. "He's the key to all that they do."

Cold Steel

The enemy commander signaled another attack while they watched. A line of soldiers trotted forward, and Brand felt the cold grip of fear in his chest, but ignored it. He was used to fighting. He would survive, or he would not, as fate and the skill of his sword arm dictated. What alarmed him was the sorcerer who stood by the shazrahad, the enemy commander. *Why hasn't he taken part in the battle?*

The deep-throated war drums of the elugs voiced a faster beat and the elugs surged.

All around him, Brand noticed his men shuffle nervously and he spoke to calm them.

"Here they come, lads. Shall we give them another warm welcome?"

Talnar one-eyed, a veteran of many battles, thrust out a scarred arm and wriggled his sword.

"Aye! With *cold* steel in their bellies!"

Other men offered different suggestions, each more descriptive than the last, and Brand laughed. Battlefield humor had a charm of its own. It was also a tool that he used as a captain: the less a soldier's tension, the better he fought.

The enemy line, a seething mass of warriors, approached. The shazrahad imposed scant order, but ferocity partially offset the lack of discipline.

Brand did not look at the faces of the enemy. Nor did he give a moment's attention to their raucous battle taunts. Both were ways to lose nerve and become intimidated. Still, sweat moistened his palms, and he gripped sword and shield tightly. The war drums beat frenetically and the elugs charged.

"Steady, lads," he said.

He waited for the right moment, as did all the captains along the line, and then gave three short blows of his whistle. He knelt like all the men while white-fletched arrows, shot from behind them, hissed overhead. Some of the enemy fell to the ground, killed outright or wounded, but their brethren charged onwards.

Again the archers shot, and this time the oncoming hoard faltered. But they did not stop. One last volley of graceful death curved through the air and then Brand gave two sharp blows of his whistle.

The men stood. Brand glanced along the line and saw that everyone had responded quickly. Their shields, now interlocked, formed a wall. Their sword arms remained free to stab.

The elugs hit them in a violent mass of screams and howls. The air turned into a crimson mist while blood sprayed and spurted. The stench of opened bowels, urine and fear filled Brand's nostrils. Yet the shield-wall held and the enemy spent themselves against it. They eventually receded like an outgoing tide, leaving the detritus of war behind: discarded weapons, broken shields, the dead and the soon-to-be-dead.

Brand gave a long and wavering whistle. The soldiers opened ranks and allowed the injured to stagger back through the newly created gaps. The same thing occurred up and down the line.

He checked his men. They looked steady and calm. Of them all, only Talnar one-eyed was dead. He lay on the ground, his single eye wide and staring, his legs drenched by blood from a wound to his upper thigh.

Brand had seen men survive axe-strokes to the head, and yet little more than the nick of a blade had felled the veteran. He gave a sigh. *Life is fragile – the chances of fate unpredictable.*

His mood swung between a sense of loss and the euphoria of survival that coursed through his body. In an attempt to settle himself, he tried to guess Gilhain's next move.

The king had intercepted the enemy and brought the battle to them instead of enduring a siege behind Cardoroth's walls. He hoped a decisive victory would ensure a long peace for his realm. It was a bold move, though not without risk.

The redheaded youth interrupted his musings.

"What's that?"

A deep noise rumbled over the fields. It came from the pine-clad hills beyond their westward flank.

Brand answered his question with a hollow whisper.

"More elugs."

"No," the youth said. "That can't be it. Hvargil's cavalry guard that flank. He sent scouts into the hills during the night and early this morning. If they were invested by the enemy, the king wouldn't have joined battle."

Brand shook his head. "Hvargil may not have told him. No matter that he never says a word out of place, there have long been rumors that he wants the crown himself. He *is* half-brother to the king."

"Even so ..." The youth's freckled face paled, "... no one would betray us like that."

Brand hesitated, but the truth was the truth.

"The war drums of the elug nation speak no lie."

The cavalry trotted north, toward the safety of Cardoroth. Brand wished he had been wrong. Not only was it a betrayal of Cardoroth's soldiers, but of Hvargil's own blood, for Gilhain would now likely die, too. Yet that same blood might see Hvargil crowned king – or start a civil war. Either way, only the city's enemies would profit.

The King

While Brand watched, the enemy emerged from gorges in the hills like a plague of rats from countless holes. They quickly formed a single line. Likewise, the original enemy to the south reformed. Cardoroth's forces were trapped, fixed like a nutshell ready for cracking between two rocks. They could stand and fight, or retreat in a rout and suffer heavy loss. All about him, men muttered and swore.

Brand looked at King Gilhain. Everything depended on how he reacted. In warfare, such changing situations ruined leaders, or brought them everlasting fame.

Gilhain was not idle. Nor did he show any sign of consternation. Swiftly but calmly he gave orders and a Durlin lifted high a carnyx horn, an ancient instrument of brass with a gold-rimmed mouth, and blew. The captains all down the line knew the signal. There would be no retreat.

Brand felt pride at how smoothly the army functioned. Responding to another blast of the horn, the line some way to his right moved. The men peeled away as though performing an orchestrated dance, and they marched quickly but unhurried to form a fresh line at a right angle to the old, establishing a new defense against that flank.

The elugs from south and west charged. The once-green grass turned to dust beneath their iron-shod boots and the war drums boomed. Menace thrummed the air.

Brand whistled and knelt. Volleys of arrows cut the doom-laden air. The charge came on and he signaled for the shield-wall. He stood upright, shoulder to shoulder with the men of Cardoroth, the leather hilt of his sword damp with sweat.

With a roar of screams, a clash of shield against shield and the ringing of swords, the opposing forces met. Brand thrust with his blade until his shoulder and wrist ached. Yet he could not stop. His shield arm grew numb from blows, and he yearned to lower it, but to do so was instant death, or worse: he would expose the man next to him.

Suddenly he sensed movement. The line began to buckle and the shield-wall to open.

He held his ground. "For Cardoroth!"

His blood burned hotly and the fire of battle surged like new life in his arms. The soldiers around him repeated his call.

"Cardoroth! Cardoroth!"

The shouts grew louder and the men remembered their courage. The shield-wall locked together; the line straightened. The renewed defiance disheartened the enemy, and they slackened their attack. Like a change in the wind, the fight went out of them and they retreated.

Brand looked about. The newly formed right wing had buckled too, and it was still under fierce assault from the fresh enemy. Yet even as he watched, the king stood tall in the flurry of battle. He knew just when to reinvigorate the men. His sword thrust, dealing swift death, and the silver helm flashed like white fire above the soldiers around him. They redoubled their efforts, refusing to be the ones who let their king down, and the line rallied. The new-formed flank tightened its line and repelled the enemy.

Gilhain returned to the rise behind the army, his helm undimmed in the sunlight, but his sword was blood-wetted and dark. He strode to his vantage point with purpose, and the Durlin surrounded him once more.

All about him Brand gazed at death. Yet the enemy had suffered the worst. It was the most brutal clash of a grisly day. The shazrahad had anticipated victory and spent the elugs in a final gambit. Now, unexpectedly beaten and weak, his forces withdrew into the hills.

Gilhain gave no order to harass the retreat, for that would have been the cavalry's task. Hvargil had rolled the dice, thought Brand, but lost. Gilhain would return victorious and his half-brother must either flee into a self-imposed exile or submit to the king's justice. The last seemed less likely.

Brand heard a new sound and tilted his head to listen. The elug war drums beat again, but their rhythm had altered. He noticed that the sorcerer and a group of elugs held their ground. It disturbed him. The men about him showed relief and rested, yet he had experience of sorcery, and the hair on his scalp lifted with fear.

The sun beat down from a cloudless sky, hot and unremitting, and nothing stirred over the field of resting warriors. Yet the stillness only served to presage dread. Something was going to happen.

The king made a gesture and a Durlin blew on the carnyx horn. It was the signal for the captains to report. Brand cleaned his sword and sheathed it but kept his hand near the hilt while he walked up the slope.

Other captains emerged along the whole line, and Brand knew what the king would order: it was time to return to Cardoroth. They would march home in victory. They had won peace, if not for a long time, at least for a while.

He walked and joined in with a score of other officers. But even as they exchanged greetings, the elug war drums pounded with heightened malice.

An eerie quiet settled over the battlefield and men's voices died in their throats. The air, heavy and oppressive, throbbed like the wild heartbeat of a beast. A shadow chilled Brand's blood even as the hot sun dimmed. He glanced up, but the azure sky remained clear. No cloud, no flock of birds, no eclipse blocked the sun; yet even so, the bright light faded as though dusk crept over the land during the middle of the day.

All about him, men's steps faltered until they stood still, caught in a net of bewilderment. But Brand knew the source of the unnaturalness, and he looked to the sorcerer. From his vantage, a little way up the slope, he saw over the heads of the bemused army and to the small group ringing the drumbeaters.

The sorcerer slowly raised his wych-wood staff. Dust stirred around his feet. The air chilled. From the cloudless sky, drops of rain, ice-cold and pregnant with foreboding, fell. They plunked on Brand's face and hands.

A single shadow coalesced in the air above the field. It took form and suddenly a swift shape of sinuous nightmare swooped toward the king's retinue.

Brand felt a surge of horror. The shadow-beast plummeted like a stooping falcon. It landed with a rush of icy air and shadow-wings. These folded back against its body, became one with it, and a giant man-shape stood before the Durlin. Its dark body thrummed with sorcerous life. Dim light glimmered faintly from the smooth dome of its head. Black hands clawed and flexed before it. It moved again, walking on mighty legs of corded shadow-muscle. Grass withered beneath the tread of its long-toed feet. Steam writhed into the air. A blackened trail smoked behind it.

A single Durlin leaped and attacked, the first test of its powers. The others held back to see what they could learn. The shadow-beast paid no heed to the bright blade that cut and stabbed its dark flesh. The strokes slid away like oil slicking over water. The massive hands snaked out and grasped the Durlin. They lifted him high, and he screamed while the shadow-beast wrung his body like a wet cloth. Blood sprayed everywhere. The creature cast aside the corpse and strode forward.

The Durlin held their ground. When it neared them they sprang as one; swords flashed, daggers flew, and men threw themselves against its legs to pull it down. But the blades did not bite, and the creature flung the grappling men away. They landed in a tangled mess of broken bones and ripped flesh.

Those who could rise leaped to attack again. But their number was halved. The king drew his own sword. Rather than flee he would face ineluctable fate with courage. Of all the Durlin, only Arawdan held back. His sword was drawn, and he stood before the king, his once-white surcoat spattered by the life-blood of his slain comrades.

Brand had seen enough. He ran, his long legs strode out, and his sword shook in his hand. He might yet reach the crest before it was too late, though what he would do, other than die with the Durlin, he did not know.

The elug war drums surged in the distance and the shadow-beast swayed and thrashed in a whirlwind of strength that threw men to the ground. Bravely, the Durlin persisted.

Men's screams pierced Brand's ears as he raced up the slope. More appalling was the noise of snapped and shattered bone. He neared as the creature slew the last of the Durlin. Only the Durlindrath and Gilhain remained.

Arawdan stepped before the king. The shadow-beast raised a great hand and struck, but the Durlindrath nimbly leapt aside and avoided the blow. His sword arm darted forward and thrust. But to no avail. The shadow-flesh turned the blade and the mighty arm returned in a backhanded blow. Once more Arawdan avoided it.

Brand, racing close, watched while Arawdan dropped his sword and drew his dagger. What was he thinking? Then Brand understood. The Durlindrath avoided yet another blow. Dexterously, he darted to the side and then leaped upon the shadow-beast's back. His left arm wrapped around the creature's neck. The dagger in his right rose and fell, seeking the beast's eyes.

The elug war drums grew frantic and the shadow-beast thrashed. Yet for all the stabbing, Brand saw no injury. He reached the creature and thrust his own sword, fast and hard, in what should have been a killing blow. The shadow-beast ignored him as it sought to dislodge Arawdan.

The war drums went silent. The creature stilled. Arawdan's blade rose and fell. The drums suddenly roared to life, and the shadow-beast dove backward, hurling itself at the ground. Too late Arawdan tried to leap away.

Caught beneath the creature, he groaned. Brand heard the snap of ribs and saw frothy blood film the Durlindrath's lips. The dagger dropped from his limp hand.

"Thrum! Thrum! Thrum!" beat the elug war drums.

The shadow-beast stood and paced toward the king. "Die! Die! Die!" it bellowed.

Brand had a sudden idea. If it did not work, wild as it was, the king was as good as dead. He hesitated, fear draining strength from his legs and sapping his will.

He glanced behind him, but the other captains had all remained where they were. There was no help there. Looking over at Arawdan, he saw that the Durlindrath yet lived. He could not move, nor speak. There was no help there, either. But his eyes implored Brand.

He hesitated no longer and picked up the discarded carnyx horn. *If this doesn't work, I'm dead.*

The horn, though six feet long, was not unwieldy. He swiftly brought the cold mouthpiece to his lips, took a deep breath, and blew for his life, for the life of the king, and for Cardoroth.

An eerie blast issued from the instrument: deep, primitive, otherworldly. It washed down the rise, over the trampled battlefield and drowned out the distant war drums. The shadow-beast faltered, its dome-like head rocked from side to side as though questing the source of a sudden pain. The very shadow-flesh of its sorcerous form quivered.

The beast bellowed and turned from the king toward Brand. Eyes, unplumbed wells of slitted hatred, bent their gaze upon him. The creature raised blood-slicked hands and lurched forward.

Brand ran out of breath and his blast on the horn ceased. *I'm going to die.*

The creature's ungainly stride gathered momentum. Brand sucked in more air and blew another blast from the horn, hugging it to him precariously with one arm until the last second. Then he struck with the blade in his other. The sword cut through shimmering flesh, severing a groping shadow-hand. Light, trapped by sorcery, blazed outward like spurting blood.

The king's blade took the creature across the back of the knees and it stumbled. It bellowed and light streamed from its mouth. The blades of king and captain struck again and again. The horn blew a third and final time. The shadow-beast, with a last desperate thrash, burst into a bright light, sharp and hot as the noonday sun, and disappeared. The elug war drums gave a loud crack while hide ripped and shriveled from their frames. The sorcerer screamed and collapsed. The drummers fled from his body.

Gilhain went to the Durlindrath, but the man's breathing had stopped. The king bowed his head.

Brand slumped to the grass and dropped his sword. The day was theirs. The king was saved; but Arawdan was dead.

Return

Brand stepped at a solemn pace. His boots echoed on the marble floor of the throne room. All the nobles of Cardoroth had gathered, their whispers echoed in the vaulted ceiling a hundred feet above. His white surcoat gleamed in the light of the sun that streamed through many skylights and windows.

He knelt before King Gilhain. The nobles hushed and Brand's voice rang out. He repeated a ritual phrase, a relic from Cardoroth's ancient past:

Tum del conar – El dar tum!
Death or infamy – I choose death!

He knew that he meant it. Otherwise, he would not have uttered the words. Arawdan had taught him what it was to be the Durlindrath: both humility and show were only masks. Courage, loyalty, cowardice and greed could reside anywhere.

The following days passed swiftly, and together with the king, Brand chose the new Durlin.

The king did not find Hvargil, though soldiers and scouts searched ceaselessly in many lands beyond Cardoroth's borders. He had exiled himself by his deeds and his infamy would resound through the years. His name became a byword for treachery, even as Arawdan's was one for loyalty.

They had achieved differing, though equal fame, yet Hvargil lived while Arawdan lay entombed in silent marble.

Brand sighed. Fate was always a roll of the dice.

7. Sample: Chapter 1 of *Raging Swords*

Brand woke. His heart thrashed in his chest. His stomach churned, and the blood in his veins ran chill. But he spared no thought for any of those things.

He lay still, wrapped in his bedclothes, while his eyes strained to see and his ears to detect whatever had roused him from forgotten dreams.

It felt cold. It was dark also, being in that last stretch of night when the hours were long and the dawn, though near, was not yet come. It was that period when the human spirit ebbed lowest, where wills were weakest and shadows pooled the most deeply.

He saw nothing out of place. He heard no noise that should not have been. Yet his heart raced ever faster, and sweat, cold and clammy, trailed down his face and onto his throat like the lingering fingers of ghosts.

All through the city a questing breeze touched and pulled and tweaked at anything loose. A weather vane creaked as it turned on some high roof. A stable door banged unheeded, and in the palace where Brand lay shivering white curtains danced palely in the open windows.

He concentrated on the breeze. He did not like it. The open window near his bed looked over the city, but he saw nothing amiss far below. Yet the air was unnaturally cold on his face. Even as the thought came to him its fluttering movement stilled. The curtains ceased their billowing, and the cobbled streets below grew quiet once more.

He let out a long breath and relaxed. All he heard now was a whisper of air down the corridor outside his room and the faint creak of doors.

The warmth under the blankets began to soothe him back to sleep. The day was not yet begun. There was no need to stir. He could rest a little while longer and gather his strength for the toils yet to come. Nor was he even wanted here, not among this foreign people. They did not like him. They did not respect him. He had spilled his blood in deadly battles to serve them, defied death for their benefit, but most would like to see his back, to see him walk off into the wild lands from whence he came.

And that was his desire – he ached to return to his homeland – to walk the paths that once he knew and to reclaim the life that had been stolen from him. Yet ties of loyalty held him, and he would not break them. The king of Cardoroth was a great man. To him he owed much, and he would serve and help in any way that he could.

Brand stirred, restless once more. Almost he had been lulled, but he knew sorcery when he felt it. Through a fog that dimmed his thoughts he forced himself to sit up in bed. His head suddenly cleared. Many in the city might wish him gone, but not the king. Gilhain trusted him. He had given him opportunity when others had not, and respect when others offered only disdain.

Gilhain! The last dregs of confusion scattered. Sorcery was afoot and the king would be its target. Brand leapt out of bed. No time he had to don chain mail or helm or the white surcoat of his station. He pulled on trousers and boots, drew the sword of his forefathers from its ancient sheath, and ran bare chested to the door.

He put his hand to the metal knob. The cold he felt there shocked him like a blow. He flung it open anyway and let go swiftly. Immediately a blast of frigid air assailed him, and as he ran the length of the corridor he saw frost on the marble floor and the iciness of it bit his unshod feet.

"Durlin!" he called loudly, summoning the king's bodyguards who slept in rooms along the passageway.

He sprinted ahead, but he saw nobody and heard no reply.

"Durlin!" he yelled again. "To the king!"

The door to Gilhain's chamber was now before him. The two Durlin stationed there lay slumped on the ground. A quick glance told him that they were dead, though no blood marked their white surcoats.

Beneath the door strange lights flickered, and he heard the first call of any person beside himself.

"Guards!" It was the queen. Fear gripped her voice and made it shrill.

A moment he hesitated, knowing that on the other side sorcery and mayhem filled the room and that he would likely die if he entered. But he was the Durlindrath, leader of the bodyguards, and when he swore his oath to protect the king he had done so from the heart.

He kicked with all his might. The door, built of sturdy oak slabs to protect against assault, did not budge. But the metal of the bolt that held it in place shattered within its icy casing. Shards from the ruined doorjamb flew into the air, and the door careened inward on its great hinges.

Brand sprang into the king's chamber. The rapid breath from his heaving chest turned to mist before him.

Yet more vapor, like a roiling fog, swirled within the room. There was no frost here, for the floor was laid with deep carpet, but ice hung in ribbons from the windows and sheeted the marble walls.

Gilhain and the queen were held at bay against the far wall. The king grasped a mighty sword in his two hands while she raised high a long knife. Six figures pressed toward them. They were wraithlike, gray and vaporous as the fog that eddied in the room. They glided on tall legs and their long arms reached forward like creeping fingers of mist toward the king's throat. The wraiths had faces: gaunt, cold-eyed and cruel. A pale light lit their hollow cheeks and glimmered silver-white in their trailing hair.

Brand had seen enough. He leaped toward them and yelled the battle cry of the Durlin: *Death or infamy!*

He attacked. His sword sliced and cut and stabbed. The wraiths were more solid than they looked, and he drew from them shuddering screams, yet their cries came as though from a great distance, and the creatures did not die. Instead of falling, three of the six turned upon him.

They reached for his throat, and one found a grip there. He felt the cold touch of death. But his sword was a Halathrin blade, forged by immortals, and though what would have been death-strokes to a man had not yet killed the wraiths, it certainly caused harm. He drove the blade forward into the closest figure until it staggered back, and then he jumped free from more reaching arms.

The creatures pressed their attack against him. And they barred the way to the king that he had sworn to protect. But they ignored the queen. And that was an error, for she fought with animal fury, and one of her deep thrusts slew a wraith whose misty form dispersed into the air with a shriek. The king, meanwhile, held the others off with deft strokes. But time was running out.

Brand swung and stabbed, holding the enemy off but not defeating them. Yet this much he had achieved: the enemy must now divide their attack that otherwise, concentrated on Gilhain alone, would by now have killed him.

He danced to the left and hewed at the outstretched arm of a foe. The blade did not sever it, but the follow up stroke drove deep into vaporish innards and Brand pushed the blade up and through to its hilt.

There was no heart to pierce, for these things drew no breath, and no blood surged through their bodies to enliven their limbs. Yet still, whatever sorcery gave them substance to kill by hand must needs also give them a physical form that might be damaged.

A moment the wraith was close to him. If it were a man they would have stood eye to eye. But in that haggard face he saw no gaze that mirrored his own. Instead, he perceived the flicker of lights and shadow coming to him as though through a fog, and he caught a sudden glimpse of a room, dark and shadow-laden, and he heard the dim sound of faraway chanting.

Before he understood whatever it was that he had heard and seen the wraith reeled back from him, but then, even as it began to sweep forward again in renewed attack, the sorcery that held it together faltered. It hissed and faded into formless vapor.

At last he heard running feet in the corridor. Light flashed from the doorway, dazzling bright. The gutted candles flared with leaping flame. The dark hearth burst with a fury of sparks and shimmering embers. Crackling flame roared to life.

Aranloth had come. He held his staff before him, and the diadem on his brow gleamed in the flaring light. The king's wizard now contended with the sorcery, and the room became furnace-hot. The sheeted ice dripped from the walls. The wraiths screeched and writhed, trying to evade the blades that now cut them with ease. Swift they died, or else sharp steel sent them back to the pit dark sorcery had conjured them from.

In the sudden silence Brand heard from afar the enemy that had laid siege to Cardoroth. From beyond the city wall the chanting of an army rose to a crescendo, but then trailed off into a din of confusion and discord. Their war drums continued to beat, holding order longer, but soon even their thrumming voices stilled.

Brand heaved for breath. Was any place now safe for the king? A host of mankind's ancient enemies gathered without, trying to break in and destroy. Yet now sorcery had slipped even inside the palace. Nowhere seemed beyond the reach of the enemy who sought Gilhain's death. And well they might, for only his brilliance and tactics had forestalled them. Without him, Cardoroth would long since have fallen, and they knew it and hated him.

Brand looked at Gilhain. It was his job, his sworn oath, to keep the man safe. And neither blade nor shaft nor poison – neither a thousand foes nor a lone assassin, not even sorcery in the night would avail against him, so long as he drew breath.

But the dead guards in the corridor reminded him that a man, no matter the strength of his will, regardless of his love and loyalty, might still be outmatched.

It was nearly so tonight. The reach of the enemy was somehow longer than it had been, and the hope of the city dwindled further. For the enemy *did* outmatch them.

The elug host was vast. The siege of Cardoroth could not be broken, and the enemy would likely prevail. If not tonight, then in a month, or six months. All the swifter if the king died, and that the enemy knew and strove to achieve – any way it could.

Brand sensed that the doom of Cardoroth was coming. By what means the enemy grew stronger rather than weaker, he could not guess. Sorcery had never yet struck so deep into the city. Always Aranloth and his like prevented it. Yet not tonight. Perhaps never again.

He saw the same understanding when he looked into Gilhain's eyes. But there was determination there also, an unflinching will, and Brand admired it.

The king might die, but if so, he would not be alone at the end.

Thus begins *Raging Swords,* book one of the Durlindrath series, wherein Brand learns more of the threat to Alithoras and faces his greatest challenge yet.

Sign up below and be the first to hear about new book releases, see previews and learn of upcoming discounts. http://eepurl.com/Rswv1

Visit my website at www.homeofhighfantasy.com

www.ingramcontent.com/pod-product-compliance
Lightning Source LLC
Chambersburg PA
CBHW022042170626
46808CB00003B/1320